Showtime
at First Baptist

by Ron Osborne

A SAMUEL FRENCH ACTING EDITION

SAMUEL
FRENCH
FOUNDED 1830

NEW YORK HOLLYWOOD LONDON TORONTO

SAMUELFRENCH.COM

IMPORTANT BILLING AND CREDIT REQUIREMENTS

All producers of *SHOWTIME AT FIRST BAPTIST must* give credit to the Author of the Play in all programs distributed in connection with performances of the Play, and in all instances in which the title of the Play appears for the purposes of advertising, publicizing or otherwise exploiting the Play and/or a production. The name of the Author *must* appear on a separate line on which no other name appears, immediately following the title and *must* appear in size of type not less than fifty percent of the size of the title type.

In addition the following credit *must* be given in all programs and publicity information distributed in association with this piece:

First produced by the Barter Theatre,
Abingdon, Virginia
by Richard Rose, Producing Artistic Director

SHOWTIME AT FIRST BAPTIST premiered on the main stage of Barter Theatre, the LORT-member State Theatre of Virginia (Richard Rose, Producing Artistic Director) in Abingdon, Virginia on June 11, 2009. It was directed by Nicholas Piper; the lighting design was by Lucas Krech; the sound design was by Bobby Beck; the costume design was by Colleen Metzger; the stage manager was Jessica Borda; and the set design was by Dan Ettinger. The cast was as follows:

EDITH	Mary Lucy Bivins
VERA	Evalyn Baron
MAE ELLEN	Amy Baldwin
OLENE	Hannah Ingram
LUCILLE	Trica Matthews
ANNIE	Katie Becker

CHARACTERS

EDITH – The pastor's spirited wife, mid-60s

VERA – The opinionated wife of the church's most powerful deacon, mid-60s

MAE ELLEN – The church's rebellious organist with a dream, 50

OLENE – A former member with a flashy past who's just returned to Ivy Gap, 50

ANNIE – A northerner living with her in-laws while her husband serves in Vietnam, early-20s

LUCILLE – Annie's mother-in-law, a tried and true Baptist, early-50s

PLACE/SET

The majority of the action takes place in the church's fellowship hall located in a fictional town in east Tennessee; several short scenes – created through the use of lighting, sound, and a chair or two – are set in a hospital waiting room and homes in Ivy Gap. The church's fellowship hall is essentially an open area furnished with several folding chairs, tables and the like. To the rear and open to the room is a small elevated stage on which there is a lectern; steps at either side of the stage lead to the elevated area. A door – which opens from the stage and leads to the church's unseen sanctuary – is upstage left. A second door exiting to an unseen hallway and the exterior of the church is down right.

TIME

April and May 1970, concurrent with the church's 100th anniversary as well as the U.S. invasion of Cambodia and the shootings at Kent State University which followed.

ACTS & SCENES

The play is divided into two acts and nine scenes (five scenes in the first act, four in the second).

MUSIC

All music specified in this script is thought by the playwright to be in the public domain.

ARTISTIC STATEMENT

Although first and foremost a comedy, ***SHOWTIME AT FIRST BAPTIST*** discusses a number of serious issues, including the conflict of religious dogma and personal conscience in a changing world, the role of women in what some may consider a closed society, and the anguish of loss.

PLAYWRIGHT'S NOTES

SHOWTIME AT FIRST BAPTIST is based on characters and situations portrayed in ***FIRST BAPTIST OF IVY GAP***, an award-winning poignant comedy that premiered on the main stage of Barter Theatre, the LORT-member State Theatre of Virginia. Subsequently, ***FIRST BAPTIST OF IVY GAP*** has been widely produced throughout the U.S and Canada.

To the loves of my life... my beautiful wife,
Melissa, and our two beautiful daughters,
Beth and Christy.

ACT I

Scene I

(The fellowship hall of the First Baptist Church of Ivy Gap. The space is decorated for a festive event, i.e., the church's gala 100th anniversary picnic which was celebrated earlier that day on the spacious grounds of the church. Hall amenities include table cloths on folding tables, potted plants, perhaps a colorful balloon or two, a photograph of Pastor Ellington, plus a banner that reads "First Baptist of Ivy Gap – 1870 – 1970.")

(At rise, we hear a mournful rendering of the traditional hymn "Go Tell It On The Mountain" *being played on an organ in the church's unseen sanctuary which is accessible via a door on the stage. If we listen carefully, we also hear a spirited bar or two from a secular song cleverly mixed in between bars of the hymn. The combination is not what we'd expect to hear in a Southern Baptist Church. After a few moments,* **EDITH** *– who has begun to pick up after the celebration – steps into the hall; she carries a folding chair in each arm. From her appearance, it's obvious she's exhausted after having coordinated the church's biggest event in its 100 years of existence.)*

EDITH. *(loudly so as to be heard over the music)* YOUR SERENADE IS LOVELY, MAE ELLEN. HOWEVER, I'D PREFER YOUR HELP IN HERE PLEASE.

*(***VERA** *– a large woman with an equally large presence sporting a large straw sun hat – enters. As she does, the music stops.)*

VERA. When I die, Edith, promise me she won't go near the Wurlitzer. As inspiring as it is, "The Hallelujah Chorus" isn't my idea of funeral music.

EDITH. Mae Ellen wouldn't dare.

VERA. Tell me please what her dancing fingers played at Louise Jennings' little going-away gathering. *(She removes her hat, then picks up a broom and joins in the clean-up effort.)*

EDITH. Was I there?

VERA. In the first row! Like the rest of us poor lost souls, searching your Baptist hymnal for words to "On The Wings Of A Snow White Dove."

EDITH. Well, she can play that thing.

VERA. And still believes someday somebody from Nashville or Knoxville or somewhere better than Ivy Gap will hear her play and make her a star. I love you to pieces, Edith. And I worry about Mae Ellen more than she worries about herself. Which is saying something! But she'd be long gone from this church without you picking up after her. Now...why are we're talking about our zealot at the keyboard when we should be talking about you...you secretive little devil? Why didn't you tell me?

(An unhappy **MAE ELLEN** *– chairs in hand – enters from the sanctuary. She hears* **VERA***'s comment.)*

MAE ELLEN. Vera. You mean you didn't know?

VERA. I had no idea –

MAE ELLEN. Well, she told *all* her friends. Didn't you, Edith?

EDITH. Don't pay attention to Mae Ellen. Charlie told the deacon board. Other than that –

MAE ELLEN. Edith. I knew something was up –

EDITH. Then you guessed. Because other than that, it was our secret –

VERA. After thirty-two years as the beloved and revered pastor of the First Baptist Church of Ivy Gap, the man is retiring...

EDITH. *Yes!* And isn't it wonderful?

VERA. *Edith!* He is taking you with him!

EDITH. Oh, you sweet thing –

VERA. I'm not sweet, and you know it. God knows, I'll miss Charlie. What will this church be without him? But you, Edith...you were –

EDITH. I was bossy. I stuck my nose in things that didn't concern me –

VERA. *All the time!* Which – for a female member of a Southern Baptist church – is godlike in my book. Not to mention, you just pulled off the best one-hundredth anniversary picnic any church ever had.

EDITH. Was it...okay? *(She knows it was.)*

VERA. Was it okay, the lady asks? *(Looking at* **MAE ELLEN** *– who has reluctantly joined the clean-up effort – for confirmation.)*

MAE ELLEN. I suppose...except for Billy Rankin's little mishap –

VERA. Any man who participates in a sack race with his suspenders unhooked ought to be exposed.

MAE ELLEN. And the Women's Bible Study tent was a bust.

VERA. Because somebody forgot the Eleventh Commandment..."Thou shall not use the words Baptist...Bible... *and Bingo* in the same sentence." Recommended by the same "somebody" who wanted our anniversary banner to read...*(pointing to the banner that hangs in the hall)* "First Baptist of Ivy Gap, *Guaranteeing* Salvation Since 1870!"

MAE ELLEN. Then there was Olene's outfit. Tongues are still wagging about that –

VERA. Something else to remember, Mae Ellen...one does not come to a Baptist picnic in the South looking like she closed a casino in Vegas.

MAE ELLEN. Olene *was* a showgirl.

VERA. And she didn't have to open her mouth to spread the word. There were those out there today who thought the devil was looking us over. For all we know about Olene and her..."exploits," maybe he was.

EDITH. Now you hush, Vera.

VERA. I'm just saying…if Olene Wiffer were a movie, she'd be banned in Ivy Gap.

(**OLENE** *enters. She sports a flashy outfit that one might wear if she closed a Vegas casino on a particularly festive Saturday night.* **VERA** *is the first to notice her entrance.*)

Speaking of…*(mouthing the words "you-know-who")*

(**EDITH, MAE ELLEN** *and* **EDITH** *look closely at* **OLENE** *and her outfit as she crosses to them.*)

OLENE. Why is everybody staring at me?

EDITH. Oh, I don't think we were staring –

OLENE. All day! Everybody staring. Like I'm a creature from another planet. Y'all need to know something… *this* is what women outside of Podunk, Tennessee wear these days! *(modeling her outfit and proud of it)* Bright, festive colors…fashionable style…fabric that clings… *(now whirling to show off the cling, seductively)* shows there's a difference in the sexes.

VERA. I believe we got that message in Genesis, Olene.

OLENE. If all *those…those…(Points to the sanctuary. Not knowing the right disparaging word.)*

EDITH. *Baptists.* You can say the word, Olene. Especially since you claim to be one of them.

OLENE. If they only knew the things going on other places –

EDITH. If you're talking about Las Vegas kinds-of-things, let's keep them our little secret. Okay?

OLENE. After twenty five years, I've come home –

VERA. Hardly "the second coming" we've been expecting, Olene.

OLENE. Diseases have been cured, man has walked on the moon…women have gone from nylons to panty hose to nothing –

VERA. Oh, I hope not.

OLENE. Yet *here*, the Middle Ages still rule! As God is my witness, Mae Ellen, I'll bring this church!…Ivy Gap!… into the 1970s! Kicking and screaming if I have to!

MAE ELLEN. Won't ever happen!

VERA. Everybody quiet, please – !

OLENE. Just you watch, Mae Ellen.

VERA. *Shhh. Everybody's here now. I have something official to say.* Our picnic today...a gala day-long affair celebrating our church's one-hundred years of dedication to the Lord...was...well, it was completely and utterly *spectacular!* Because of one very special lady...*take a bow, Edith Ellington!*

(**VERA** *turns to* **EDITH** *who is embarrassed and does not bow.* **VERA** *and* **OLENE** *applaud enthusiastically;* **MAE ELLEN** *is less demonstrative.*)

EDITH. You know I had all kinds of help.

OLENE. No, no, Vera's right! *(looks at* **VERA,** *critically)* For once.

VERA. God knows, Edith, I haven't had this much fun since Harry and I parked the kids at his folks and camped on top of Old Smokey. Keep it to yourself, Olene.... that night, *our sleeping bag* was sending out signals.

OLENE. Edith, sit. You deserve it. *(unfolds one of the chairs, slides it behind* **EDITH***)*

EDITH. Thank you, Olene. *(takes a seat, then a deep breath)* I don't mind telling you I prayed for good weather –

VERA. Sixty-five beautiful degrees. Some nasty-looking weather moving in, but late in the day. Prayer answered.

EDITH. After dreaming our picnic was potluck and everybody brought a lime Jell-O salad, I prayed even harder we wouldn't run out of chicken or potato salad or any of a dozen other fried, salty, super sweet things –

VERA. Say it, Edith...all those "bad-for-ya goodies" Baptists expect to greet them at the pearly gates.

EDITH. We had enough of everything to feed the whole Soviet army!

VERA. Which surely would've had better manners than our rowdy collection of famished Bible-thumpers.

MAE ELLEN. *(to* **OLENE,** *caustically)* Known locally as the "Praise-the-Lord-and-pass-the-beans" crowd.

VERA. Truth be told, Edith…there hasn't been this much bumping and shoving in Ivy Gap since Myrtle Johnson claimed Elvis was buying bananas at the Piggly-Wiggly.

EDITH. And I prayed for something else…

VERA. Oh…?

EDITH. I prayed Charlie's retirement announcement wouldn't make me melt all over myself.

VERA. Well, two out of three isn't bad.

MAE ELLEN. You cried like a baby.

OLENE. You did, Edith.

EDITH. I know. I almost drowned in my own tears!

VERA. Of course you did. Charlie's been an institution at First Baptist for ages. It's sad…scary even, to think about walking away from everything.

EDITH. I cried because I was so…*incredibly happy! (stands, obviously still very happy)*

VERA. Not *that* happy I hope.

EDITH. I'll see the world. The two of us will. We'll go places, do things…*exciting things* I've been afraid to dream because I didn't think they could come true. *(claps, bubbling with joy, becoming more animated)* Oh, can you believe it? We've already signed up for an ocean cruise. The handsome Pastor Ellington and his admiring bride of three decades-plus are sailing all the way to the Bahama Islands.

OLENE. Good for you, Edith!

EDITH. The cruise part's scary I know. But, I'm a Baptist… I can swim. And hallelujah…Edith Ellington has attended her last committee meeting! She is through watching smart, capable folks who – by themselves – could do wondrous things…become dumber than dirt in the company of others.

VERA. As I've always said, Edith…"God so loved the world, he did not send a committee."

EDITH. *(continuing to be caught up in the joyous moment)* Plus my heels are out, my flats are in. No longer will I fix an extra-special dinner, then eat by my lonesome because Charlie's off holding hands somewhere. *(Pauses, smiling seductively.)* And who knows, Vera? I may even read a trashy book.

MAE ELLEN. What's new about that?

EDITH. *Without* the plain brown wrapper.

VERA. *Edith!*

EDITH. And Charlie! He'll trade his preacher's robe for forty acres and a pair of overalls. The poor, dear man – who can't tell a tomato from a turnip – wants to be a gentleman farmer!

VERA. He cultivated God's garden for thirty years. He must've learned something.

EDITH. Just in case, I'm surprising him with an addition to his collection of sermons...a lifetime subscription to "Successful Farming." *(horrified for failing to acknowledge what her church and friends have meant to her.)* Oh, Lord. Look at me. I'm sounding so ungrateful.

OLENE. We understand.

VERA. Speak for yourself, Olene.

EDITH. I wouldn't change the last thirty-two years for anything! I got to watch Charlie grow...become the amazing man of God I knew he'd be the moment he got called. Along the way I got to sit back –

VERA. The Edith Ellington I knew didn't do much sitting.

EDITH. I met the most marvelous folks in the world...my Ivy Gap family. Especially the three of you.

VERA. We go back a long way, Edith.

OLENE. Remember rolling surgical bandages during the war–?

VERA. Planning celebrations when nobody else seemed to care–?

EDITH. Oh, we cried together...laughed together. So many memories! I wouldn't change a minute of any of it for anything.

(**EDITH** – *realizing* **MAE ELLEN***'s having a hard time – smiles caringly at* **MAE ELLEN***, then reaches for her hand.*)

EDITH. Now, however, I'm ready to do something different in the time I've got left with the incredible man God blessed me with all those years ago. I'll admit, though, there are moments I feel guilty about walking away from everything.

VERA. We're Baptists, Edith. We're suppose to feel guilty about things we've haven't even *thought* about doing. Come here, you sweet thing...let me hug your neck.

(**VERA** *hugs* **EDITH**. **OLENE** *also steps to* **EDITH**, *first smiling then embracing her warmly.* **MAE ELLEN** – *who has tears in her eyes – keeps her distance. We hear a clap of thunder.*)

OLENE. Are you okay, Mae Ellen?

MAE ELLEN. Smoke from the men's auxiliary barbeque...in my eyes still –

VERA. Ah, yes. Hamburgers three-ways. Take your pick... medium burned, burned and well burned.

EDITH. Speaking of men, Mae Ellen...I believe you spent the better part of the day talking to Lloyd Baxter.

VERA. Bigger news than that. She shared a slice of Norma Foster's prize-winning pecan pie with him...(*raising her eyebrows, seductively*) *One* fork.

OLENE. (*to* **MAE ELLEN**) Who needs spies when we've got them.

VERA. I know I should keep my mouth shut. But if you're still looking for love, Mae Ellen – and the Lord knows you are – you're climbing the wrong Magnolia –

EDITH. Shhh. If it's something that shouldn't be said –

VERA. She should know, Edith.

MAE ELLEN. Know what?

VERA. The handsome Lloyd Baxter you wrapped yourself around this afternoon –

MAE ELLEN. What about him?

VERA. He's engaged.

MAE ELLEN. That's not true.

VERA. It is. And I hear she's a hard combination to top…a good-looking, sweet-talking Methodist with money.

(We hear another clap of thunder – one that's a good deal closer; **MAE ELLEN** *angrily turns and crosses to exit.)*

EDITH. Mae Ellen…

VERA. Mae Ellen, please! At times like this, you need to remember something…men think they're the apple of God's eye when, in fact, they're the constant pain in our rear ends.

(Without looking back, **MAE ELLEN** *steps through the doorway into the unseen sanctuary.)*

OLENE. Why did you have to tell her he was engaged?

EDITH. Vera…tsk.

VERA. *(looking to the heavens, angry at herself)* Oh, Lord! Everything about me keeps getting bigger…*especially* my mouth.

(We hear another crack of thunder, followed by the sounds of **MAE ELLEN** *back at her Wurlitzer. She plays a bitter, caustic version of* "The Battle Hymn of the Republic," *one that reflects her current feelings of rejection. Moments later, we hear another even louder bolt of thunder; suddenly* **MAE ELLEN** *'s organ sounds a crashing wrong cord.* **OLENE,** **VERA** *and* **EDITH** *look at one another. A moment later we hear a scream from the sanctuary.* **EDITH** *immediately runs up the steps on to the stage, dashes to the door leading to the sanctuary, flings it open. She looks in and is horrified by the sight.)*

EDITH. *Oh, my God! NO!*

(BLACKOUT)

End of Scene

Scene II

(The church's fellowship hall, the next day. Simply stated, the space is a mess...tables, chairs, plants, deflated balloons, etc., are scattered about. The "First Baptist" banner that proudly decorated the room at the beginning of the play now hangs by a thread or two from its mount. Many things have changed in the interim; unfortunately, those we see before us are but the tip of the iceberg.)

*(At rise, the hall is empty. After a few moments, **VERA** enters through the side door; again she wears a hat which we begin to recognize as her trademark. The smell of stale smoke in the air and the appearance of the room shock her. In an effort to clear the air, she waves her hand in front of her face. After another moment, she spots the banner, steps to it, attempts to return it to its former position. As she does, **MAE ELLEN** enters from what was the sanctuary. Without a word – and with **VERA** watching – she closes the door, solemnly steps down from the stage and crosses to **VERA**; there she picks up a chair, deliberately unfolds it and sits.)*

VERA. *(pointing to the sanctuary)* I don't want to look in there, do I...?

*(A dejected **MAE ELLEN** mutters something, shaking her head as she does.)*

Your organ...it's...?

*(**MAE ELLEN** understands the question; by virtue of **MAE ELLEN**'s silence, **VERA** knows the answer.)*

Mae Ellen, I'm sorry. I know how much it meant to you.

MAE ELLEN. Do you?

*(**MAE ELLEN** shakes her head repeatedly. After a moment, **OLENE** enters through the side door. Her attire today is a tad more conservative. She sees **MAE ELLEN**, quickly steps to her, attempts to embrace her. **MAE ELLEN** isn't about to be consoled.)*

OLENE. *(now turning back to* **VERA**, *bitterly)* *HOW COULD THIS HAPPEN?*

VERA. Don't shout at me, Olene.

OLENE. One moment we're celebrating the church's 100th anniversary. Everybody's smiling, laughing. We're having the time of our lives. The next, there's a bolt of lightning. It hits the steeple...*with a cross on top, for God's sake – !*

VERA. Shame on you, Olene!

OLENE. There's fire. Smoke is everywhere. In a wink, the sanctuary – the heart of the church – it's gone! *And it's the only thing that is.* Explain it to me, Vera. Because I don't think I understand!

VERA. I can't explain it to you, Olene.

OLENE. So there *is* an explanation, huh? In the Bible some-where? *Well, what is it?*

*(***VERA** *makes no offer to explain.)*

Obviously, we can't ask Charlie. He's in the hospital. *(Looking at* **VERA**, *her hands on her hips, angrily.)* I WANT AN ANSWER!

(After a moment, **EDITH** *enters. All eyes are on her as she crosses in silence to the others. She pauses before speak-ing.)*

EDITH. He's doing...okay I think. In fact, I believe Charlie's doing a whole lot better than anybody expected.

VERA. Praise God!

(Led by **VERA**, *the women take turns hugging* **EDITH**.*)*

EDITH. I knew you'd be here. So I thought I'd come by... give y'all a full report...in person. Oh, Lord. Look at this room.

VERA. Forget the room, Edith. Tell us more about Charlie.

EDITH. Okay. All right. He's got some burns...on his right hand and arm, running up to his elbow almost. Fortu-nately, his doctors – who are wonderful – claim they're mostly superficial.

VERA. Hallelujah!

EDITH. And he...inhaled some smoke. So he's on oxygen. And reasonably comfortable I think.

VERA. You'll tell us when we can visit.

EDITH. *(nods, while doing her best to hold back tears)* This morning he was able to squeeze my hand –

VERA. That's good news, Edith!

EDITH. His doctors think so too.

(Silence as **VERA, OLENE** *and* **MAE ELLEN** *study an unsteady, fearful* **EDITH.**)

VERA. You won't ask, so I will...how can we help?

EDITH. Oh, Lord...I don't know, Vera. Follow me around maybe. Remind me to put a tea bag in my cup. Which I forgot this morning. Help me find my car. Which was missing until I remembered I left it at the hospital last night. The only thing I did all day that made any sense was pray.

VERA. That's what everybody in Ivy Gap is doing.

EDITH. Even the Presbyterians, I understand.

VERA. The Methodists have offered their sanctuary for services.

EDITH. No more Methodist jokes, Vera.

VERA. And the insurance people have been called. Before we know it, rebuilding will begin. Everything'll be shinning like new.

OLENE. Isn't it wonderful, Vera? What money can do?

(An awkward silence as **EDITH** *in particular considers Charlie's plight.* **MAE ELLEN** *breaks the silence.)*

MAE ELLEN. Do you know what I think, Edith?

EDITH. What is that, Mae Ellen?

MAE ELLEN. I think he's a hero.

EDITH. If you're talking about Charlie, you know he wouldn't agree –

VERA. Mae Ellen was there!

MAE ELLEN. Edith. He rushed in –

VERA. The fire was way out of control by then.

MAE ELLEN. He ran straight to the altar –

VERA. He grabbed the church records!

MAE ELLEN. He saved them, Edith!

VERA. He saved you too, Mae Ellen!

EDITH. Well…if that's true –

MAE ELLEN. It is, Edith!

EDITH. Then I suppose that's Charlie for you.

OLENE. Of course, if yesterday hadn't been the church's centennial –

VERA. But it was, Olene.

OLENE. The church's registry wouldn't have been on display. It would've been in a fireproof safe…*protected*. Charlie wouldn't have had to –

VERA. Olene, please! God works in mysterious ways.

OLENE. I am *so* tired of hearing that every time something goes wrong!

(OLENE sneers at VERA as EDITH surveys the others; all – including EDITH – look equally dejected.)

EDITH. Look at us…

(The four women look at one another. At the moment, they're not a pretty sight.)

Overnight we've turned into one sad-looking group. Isn't that right, Mae Ellen?

MAE ELLEN. My organ is gone, Edith!

EDITH. And Charlie's a sick man. And Olene's unhappy with God. And Vera – I'm sorry, Vera – but like always, you're at war with men.

VERA. They started it, Edith.

EDITH. So…then…why don't we just stand around and moan?

(Silence as the women again look at one another and all but moan.)

EDITH. Or maybe – just maybe – we could try putting things back together. *(She begins to pick up the room, starting with chairs which she picks up and places [folded] against a wall.)* Well, don't just stand there!

(OLENE and VERA take the cue and begin picking up the room. Only MAE ELLEN remains in place.)

We could use your help, Mae Ellen.

(Reluctantly, MAE ELLEN joins the pick-up effort. In a wink or two, the hall has been restored to some semblance of order after which there's another awkward silence.)

MAE ELLEN. So...now...what, Edith?

EDITH. Well...let's...think about that for a moment. *(pause)* Your want your organ replaced. That'll take money. Right? *(silence)* And the church's spirits need to be raised. That's for sure. Right? *(another silence)* Well, I believe we're the folks to do something about both of these important things –

MAE ELLEN. Raising money and raising spirits?

EDITH. At the same time...why not?

MAE ELLEN. Okay. But...what...? *(silence)* Edith...?

EDITH. At the moment, Mae Ellen, I'm afraid I haven't the foggiest idea. *(Looking to the heavens.)* However, I have faith God will show us the way. Just as I know... *(Closes her eyes, bows her head, with feeling.)*...he'll watch over Charlie.

(OLENE, VERA and MAE ELLEN – all somewhat confused – look at one another. They bow their heads in unison as the lights slowly dim to black.)

End of Scene

Scene III

(The church's fellowship hall, several days later. The appearance of the space is unchanged.)

*(At rise, **EDITH** enters through the door from the parking area. She struggles with a cake that's lavishly decorated with chocolate icing and extra-large pink flowers.)*

EDITH. *(to herself, surprised no one else is in the hall)* Obviously, they didn't know I'd be bringing a cake.

*(**EDITH** places the cake on a table. After a moment, she crosses slowly to the stage area of the set, walks up the steps. We know she'd like to open the door to what's left of the sanctuary but doesn't. Instead, she turns, steps to the lectern, places her hands on it, then lowers her head on to her hands. One might reasonably guess she's saying a prayer.)*

*(**VERA** enters; she wears another in her wardrobe of hats, this one a tad more colorful. She sees **EDITH** at the lectern but says nothing. Moments later, **MAE ELLEN** enters. They observe **EDITH** in thoughtful silence.)*

VERA. Edith. Are you all right?

EDITH. *(looking up, startled, a bit embarrassed)* Of course, I'm all right.

VERA. Nothing's happened I hope...?

EDITH. I just left the hospital. Charlie's doing...he's doing pretty much the same – thank you.

VERA. Then why are you standing up there, looking like tomorrow's not coming?

EDITH. I was just...thinking –

VERA. *(not buying it)* Just thinking, huh?

*(**OLENE** enters. She remains by the door, listening.)*

EDITH. About what Charlie might say if he were here.

MAE ELLEN. Since you wrote most of his sermons –

EDITH. That's not true, Mae Ellen.

MAE ELLEN. I heard your voice in his preaching for thirty years.

EDITH. I may have planted an idea or two –

VERA. Shhh. Before the deacon board hears somebody wearing a skirt contributed to a Southern Baptist worship service.

OLENE. *(now stepping to the edge of the stage, looking up at* **EDITH***)* So what *would* he say, Edith? *(silence)* Edith! I'm interested – I'd like to know.

EDITH. I think, Olene, he'd start by telling us that God isn't angry at us.

OLENE. Whew! That's a relief.

EDITH. Do you want to hear or not?

OLENE. I'm listening…

EDITH. He'd also tell us He didn't send His wrath down on us because of something we did or didn't do –

OLENE. Or what I wore to the picnic.

EDITH. Or what you wore to the picnic.

OLENE. In spite of what everybody's saying?

EDITH. In spite of what a few silly people who don't know what they're talking about are saying, yes. And he'd want us to rejoice that nobody died…that we still have a place to gather. He'd remind us that what was destroyed can be fixed.

MAE ELLEN. Including the Wurlitzer?

EDITH. Why do you think we'll be raising money? And he'd tell us – especially me – to quit mulligrubbing…to get about our business. Finally – knowing Charlie – he'd promise everything we've gone through will make us stronger. Maybe even help us do things we never imagined we could do. *(after a moment, forcing a smile)* That's what I think he'd say, Olene.

VERA. Of course, it would've taken him an hour and a half to say it.

(Led by **VERA***, the women gently applaud* **EDITH***'s "sermon." Immediately, we hear a siren. The sound grows louder until it's as if it were just outside the hall.)*

OLENE. *WHAT'S THAT?*

(OLENE rushes to the door leading to the exterior of the church, opens it. Only OLENE appears excited about the sound.)

OLENE. *(looking out)* It's a lady –

MAE ELLEN. A word to the wise, Olene…some things aren't as they appear.

OLENE. *Driving a big red Cadillac Coupe de Ville* –

MAE ELLEN. With a siren –

OLENE. *On the fender!*

MAE ELLEN. And flashing lights –

OLENE. *On the roof!*

MAE ELLEN.	**VERA.**
We know!	*We know!*

(The siren sound ends and OLENE steps away from the door. After a moment, LUCILLE enters. She sees OLENE and steps to her.)

LUCILLE. Well, now! Look at who's greeting me at the door of *my* church. "The Queen of the Night" herself!

EDITH. Her name is Olene Wiffer, Lucille.

LUCILLE. No, no, Edith. I have heard on the highest authority this…*person* – who I may have known in another lifetime and have avoided like the plague for the two weeks she's been back – was regularly introduced with significant fanfare in despicable places we don't talk about in Ivy Gap as "Madam Midnight…" *(taking a better look at OLENE and her figure; not impressed)* Hmmm. Perhaps I do have the wrong person here…

OLENE. Oh, no you don't! 'Cause here she is…in person… *(rushes to the stage, then with full dramatics)* The Queen of the Night…*MADAM MIDNIGHT* –

EDITH. *(She can guess what's coming.)* Close your eyes, Lucille!

OLENE. *And her TREASURE CHEST! (shakes her chest, suggesting more is coming)*

EDITH. *Don't you dare!*

OLENE. Edith! I've got a reputation to save .. !

EDITH. *Not in here, you don't!*

(**OLENE** *stops doing her "thing," looks at* **LUCILLE**. *The two women face off at one another for a long moment.*)

MAE ELLEN. *(sarcastically)* Olene, meet the one and only Lucille Spears.

LUCILLE. Get it right, Mae Ellen. Lucille Spears, assistant deputy police chief of Ivy Gap.

MAE ELLEN. Her husband's mayor, so –

LUCILLE. Oh, I hope you're not implying. Because without your blasphemy on the organ, none of this awfulness would've happened –

EDITH. Shame on you, Lucille!

LUCILLE. She offended God, Edith!

MAE ELLEN. God sent the lightning *because of me?*

LUCILLE. I don't know how God works, but I *do* know, Mae Ellen, your organ is *toasted.*

MAE ELLEN. *WHY YOU…!* (*takes a couple of steps toward* **LUCILLE**)

EDITH. (*picking up her cake, hoping to distract the combatants*) EVERYBODY…look what I've got…

OLENE. (*as angry as* **MAE ELLEN**) Not now, Edith! I also have something to say!

EDITH. Oh, Lord, help us.

OLENE. Just because you have a siren on your gaudy red Cadillac – what is that all about anyway? It doesn't give you the right to be the moral authority of Ivy Gap or anywhere else.

MAE ELLEN. Way to go, Olene!

OLENE. I've done something with my life…you may not have liked what it was…but it brightened peoples' lives, put smiles on their faces –

LUCILLE. Oh, I'm sure it did!

OLENE. I'm proud of what I've accomplished…artistically and financially. And no closed-minded, self-important, small-town –

LUCILLE. *You sold yourself to men!*

OLENE. *I never sold myself to any man!*

LUCILLE. *Well, you certainly sold yourself to the Devil!*

OLENE. *How dare you – !*

EDITH. STOP...!

(It's obvious OLENE, MAE ELLEN and LUCILLE have lots more to say as they face off at one another.)

All of you now! Calm down – take a deep breath! This is still a church...*if* you can believe it.

(Silence as OLENE and LUCILLE continue to sneer at one another. In an effort to be funny, MAE ELLEN breaks the silence.)

MAE ELLEN. Anybody want a piece of cake?

EDITH. *(a command) Everybody...have* a piece of cake!

(VERA picks up the sheet cake, looks at the inscription on it.)

VERA. What's this, Edith?

EDITH. *(Finding paper plates, forks, napkins.)* Whatdaya think it is? It's a cake.

VERA. The inscription..."Happy Birthday, Lionel." Who's Lionel?

MAE ELLEN. Lionel...who-didn't-want-pink-flowers-on-his-birthday-cake...Lionel. Am I right, Edith?

VERA. Edith bought a reject!

EDITH. I did. And Charlie would be proud of me – I saved a bundle. *(now serving the cake to the others)* Now, everybody...*eat!*

(Silence as everybody takes a bite, whether they want to or not.)

LUCILLE. May I say something...?

EDITH. Haven't you said enough for one morning, Lucille?

LUCILLE. Maybe I did come on a little strong to Mae Ellen and...*(points to OLENE without looking at her)* her.

EDITH. What's her name?

LUCILLE. It's...it's Olene. *(managing to look at OLENE)* You should know, normally I don't act like this...

(**MAE ELLEN** *raises her eyebrows as if to say, "not true."*
LUCILLE *knows what* **MAE ELLEN**'s *reaction is without looking.*)

LUCILLE. Well, I don't, Mae Ellen! It's just this morning the mail came. And there wasn't a letter for me from David –

EDITH. *(calmly explaining things to* **OLENE**, *hoping to ease the tension)* David is Lucille's son. He's in the army.

LUCILLE. Of course, Annie got two letters –

EDITH. Annie is Lucille's daughter-in-law. She's from Wisconsin. She's staying with Lucille and Wallace –

MAE ELLEN. You remember Wallace...the mayor.

EDITH. While David's in –

OLENE. The army. I got the picture, Edith.

LUCILLE. Plus, driving over here I had the regrettable misfortune of encountering that strange Reverend Taylor –

VERA. The new Episcopal priest in town.

EDITH. Who I assure you, Lucille, is a very nice person.

LUCILLE. Edith – please! His church is thinking about ordaining women.

VERA. And that's a problem because...?

LUCILLE. As has been my habit for thirty-plus years, Vera...I will pray for you. Now – as I was saying – this man was driving all of forty-five in a thirty-mile zone. So – as the assistant deputy police chief of Ivy Gap and vicinity – it was my duty to do something. So, I honked my horn... flashed my lights –

MAE ELLEN. On her gaudy red Cadillac Coupe de Ville –

EDITH. Hush, Mae Ellen.

LUCILLE. Well, he still wouldn't pull over. So, naturally I did what any self-respecting lady of the law heading for someplace important would do. I crept up to within an inch of his bumper, flipped my siren on "full blast." As I flew by him – his dinky little Plymouth sitting in the ditch on the side of the road – I witnessed...horror of horrors!...The most vulgar gesture ever perpetrated by a so-called man of the cloth –

MAE ELLEN. He was just pointing to Heaven, Lucille.

LUCILLE. Well, he's going to Hell, Mae Ellen.

MAE ELLEN. Or maybe God's sending *you* a message...don't mess with Episcopalians.

LUCILLE. What I'm saying is...if I've said something wrong this morning, blame the Reverend.

(**EDITH** *also looks at* **OLENE** *who's still smoldering from her encounter with* **LUCILLE.**)

EDITH. Olene...

OLENE. *What?*

EDITH. I believe Lucille's trying to apologize.

LUCILLE. I believe I *have* apologized, Edith.

EDITH. Maybe, Olene, you could...say something –

OLENE. Edith! *Even* in Las Vegas, people say they're "sorry."

LUCILLE. If it makes you happy...I'm...*(can't seem to get it out)...*

EDITH. Say it, Lucille.

LUCILLE. All right! I'm sorry – *even* if that's what they say in...*(These words are also hard for her to say, shuddering.)* ...out there.

EDITH. Now, that that's settled. Some of us need to get down to business.

LUCILLE. That's exactly why I was rushing over here.

EDITH. Oh...?

VERA. *(apologetically, to* **EDITH**) I guess maybe I mentioned something to her about the little *committee* you're –

EDITH. Uh-uh, Vera. We don't say that word anymore.

VERA. The little...*group* you're forming.

LUCILLE. Whatever you want to call it, Edith...as a God-fearing, full-fledged Baptist of more years than I care to announce...I immediately said to myself, I must be a part of it too. Oh, I do hope that's okay with every-body?

(Judging by **OLENE** *and* **MAE ELLEN** *'s reaction,* **LUCILLE** *'s involvement isn't all right with them.)*

LUCILLE. And I'd like very much if Annie could join us as well. I'm afraid she's not finding much to entertain her in Ivy Gap –

OLENE. Can you imagine?

LUCILLE. Plus she's coming up empty looking for a job. Unless you call waiting tables at that dreadful Dixie Dew Diner a job. Which is off limits, of course. So being here with y'all…it'll make her feel like she's part of things.

EDITH. Well, I suppose it'll be all right…

(**MAE ELLEN** and **OLENE** shake their heads, an action unseen by **LUCILLE.**)

LUCILLE. Wonderful. Because between us, the poor Yankee child, bless her heart, seems to believe life should be like an oven pop-over…cooked on high and eaten in a wink. When all of us down here know it should be like grits…slow cooked, seasoned with salt, butter and love…then served on grandma's hand-me-down china. After the proper Baptist blessing, of course.

(**MAE ELLEN, VERA,** and **OLENE** bow their heads and automatically say "Amen" as a young and pretty **ANNIE** enters, stopping just inside the door. Her speech pattern is definitely not Southern. She's either very self-confident or putting on a very good show.)

ANNIE. Hi, everybody. I'm Annie.

LUCILLE. Come in…let me introduce you. Since you are now officially a part of our little…*group* here.

ANNIE. From your descriptions, Mrs. Spears, I believe I know everybody.

LUCILLE. I've asked the child a thousand times to call me Lucille.

ANNIE. (*extending her hand to* **EDITH**) You're Mrs. Ellington I bet.

EDITH. (*taking* **ANNIE**'s *hand*) "The oldest looking woman in the room."

LUCILLE. Those words never flowed through my lips, Edith.

EDITH. Unfortunately, they flow through my mind on a regular basis. Especially when I see myself looking at myself.

VERA. Ah, yes...mirror, mirror on the wall...who's the fairest of 'em all? Try saying that while tugging on a bathing suit.

EDITH. Welcome to First Baptist of Ivy Gap, Annie. I'm afraid Mother Nature decided our sanctuary needed "remodeling" more desperately than Vera and I do.

ANNIE. I know all about Pastor Ellington. I'm sure he'll be okay. And the two of you look just fine to me, Mrs. Elllington.

EDITH. This is really your daughter-in-law, Lucille?

LUCILLE. I'm doing my best to change her, Edith.

ANNIE. Of course, I know Mrs. Reynolds. Who everybody knows lives next door to Mr. and Mrs. Spears.

VERA. *(to ANNIE)* We've been neighbors since I was your age. See what it's done to me?

LUCILLE. It's true. Once upon a time Vera Reynolds was the Elizabeth Taylor of Ivy Gap.

VERA. And now I'm the what...? The Doris Day maybe. The − ?

LUCILLE. I am through labeling people.

VERA. Really, Lucille. I'd like to know.

EDITH. She lies, Lucille. She doesn't want to know.

VERA. Edith, please! I'm a big girl now.

LUCILLE. *Ma Kettle!*

VERA. *You are mud, Lucille Spears!*

LUCILLE. The vision of you tugging on that bathing suit, wearing one of those ridiculous hats your parade around in. I mean −

VERA. Criticize *me* all you want. I do enough of that myself. *But leave my hats alone or so help me...!*

(EDITH holds up her hand as a signal to LUCILLE and VERA to stop their insults. Although it's difficult for

them, they do. **EDITH** *speaks calmly.*)

EDITH. Your mother-in-law, Annie, is a wonderful Christian lady. And Vera is a rock of this church whose friendship I've cherished since the Old Testament was new. Put them in the same room, however. Allow them to open their mouths...it's like David and Goliath are alive and well and calling Ivy Gap home. Now, Annie, you were saying...

ANNIE. *(smiles at* **EDITH**, *steps to* **MAE ELLEN**) I was saying, I bet you're Mae Ellen.

MAE ELLEN. Oh, I am dying to hear what...*(looks at* **LUCILLE**) she said about me.

ANNIE. She said you play beautiful music.

*(***LUCILLE**, *unseen by* **MAE ELLEN**, *shakes her head, indicating that* **ANNIE***'s words are a far cry from those she's used to describe* **MAE ELLEN** *and/or her music.)*

MAE ELLEN. Really?

*(***LUCILLE** *stops shaking her head just as* **MAE ELLEN** *looks in her direction.)*

ANNIE. *(to* **OLENE**) And you're the brave lady who left Ivy Gap years ago and just came back after what sounds like a most interesting career in show business. I want to know everything.

LUCILLE. Annie, please! Even Lutherans like you don't want to know everything about *that* everything.

ANNIE. Who knows, Mrs. Spears. I may decide to follow in her footsteps.

(Of course, **LUCILLE** *is horrified at the suggestion.)*

OLENE. I go by lots of names, Annie, but I prefer Olene.

ANNIE. Olene...

EDITH. Well, now! Everybody's met everybody. And miracle of miracles – we've gotten along for one whole minute. So...put on your thinking caps... let us begin.

ANNIE. I'm not very good at coming up with ideas, Mrs. Ellington.

EDITH. Then you're in the right place, sweetie.

VERA. Speaking for myself, I haven't had an original thought since I started coloring my hair. *(thinks about what she's just said)* Or was it the day I married Harry?

OLENE. Raising money and raising spirits...that's what we're after. Right?

EDITH. Uh-huh. And there are no bad ideas –

OLENE. Casino night at First Baptist –

EDITH. Bad idea. Next...

VERA. A ladies luncheon and fashion show...

OLENE. Only if I'm in charge of the fashions.

EDITH. More ideas...come on...let me hear...

ANNIE. A really big dinner and dance...

LUCILLE. A reminder, my dear...Southern Baptists don't dance.

OLENE. Speak for yourself. *(She does a step or two, while looking at* **LUCILLE.***)*

VERA. A bridge tournament...

MAE ELLEN. Car washes...bake sales...

VERA. Pot luck dinners.

EDITH. We're trying to raise spirits, not put people to work.

MAE ELLEN. A benefit show.

EDITH. Tell me more ..

MAE ELLEN. Well...I suppose we would...*(coming up empty)*

EDITH. I'm listening, Mae Ellen...

MAE ELLEN. I don't know, Edith! I guess we'd...hire singers, musicians...charge admission –

LUCILLE. A gospel concert! What a wonderful idea!

EDITH. Hire? You mean we'd spend money to make money.

OLENE. That's America, Edith. But a gospel concert... *(yawns at the idea)*

MAE ELLEN. Of course, we have our own talent right here...

EDITH. In our church, you mean?

MAE ELLEN. Well, sure. Olene can...*(She wiggles as if dancing, looking at* **LUCILLE** *as she moves.)* And I play the piano. And Vera can –

VERA. Vera can sit and watch others make fools of themselves. Which isn't to say that once upon a time I didn't
dream of finding myself on Broadway…singing, dancing… *(She moves as if she were on Broadway, before catching
herself.)* Which is something that will never leave this
room.

MAE ELLEN. If we do it ourselves it wouldn't cost us anything.

OLENE. Now, this is beginning to sound like fun.

EDITH. That's the whole idea!

LUCILLE. I don't know, Edith. *(obviously unhappy with the
whole idea)*

ANNIE. Well, I think it's a terrific idea

EDITH. And Charlie'll love it. Except we'll need a name.

OLENE. For the show, you mean?

EDITH. If we're going to sell it, sure –

LUCILLE. Edith, First Baptist of Ivy Gap is in the business
of saving souls. This sounds like show business to me.

OLENE. What do you think church is?

EDITH. Careful, Olene.

MAE ELLEN. I don't have a name for the show. But I've got
one for us I think.

EDITH. Our little planning group…our gang of six you
mean?

MAE ELLEN. Uh-huh. Except it isn't real catchy. In fact, I
don't think anybody would remember it.

OLENE. So, tell us… *(silence)*

EDITH. Mae Ellen…? *(another silence)*
Mae Ellen, we are waiting!

MAE ELLEN. All right! How about… *(beat)* How about…
Charlie's Angels.

*(Everyone looks at **EDITH**, who's been caught off guard
by **MAE ELLEN**'s suggestion. Tears well in her eyes as the
lights dim to black.)*

End of Scene

Scene IV

(It's a couple of days later. Initially, we see a hospital waiting room [created downstage right through the use of lighting and sound plus several chairs arranged in a row]).

(At rise, a light comes up on **EDITH** *who sits in one of the aforementioned chairs. She picks up a magazine, opens it, then – almost as quickly – loses interest and closes it. As she does, we hear a doctor's name paged on the hospital's public address system. After a moment, a reserved* **MAE ELLEN** *enters. She sees a deeply concerned* **EDITH** *and steps to her.)*

MAE ELLEN. They said I'd find you here.

EDITH. *(looking up, surprised)* Mae Ellen...

MAE ELLEN. I was down the street. I thought I'd come by.

EDITH. Still no visitors in his room – I'm sorry.

MAE ELLEN. Then I'll just have to keep you company. Okay?

EDITH. It's sweet of you to come, Mae Ellen. Thank you.

*(***MAE ELLEN*** sits aside* **EDITH***. There's a brief awkward silence.)*

MAE ELLEN. I don't imagine anything's changed...?

EDITH. I'm waiting to see his doctor now.

MAE ELLEN. You know, Edith...if prayers mean anything –

EDITH. You know they do, Mae Ellen.

*(***MAE ELLEN*** nods. Another period of silence follows during which* **EDITH** *senses she's not the only who's troubled.)*

We're not doing so good, are we, sweetie?

MAE ELLEN. I don't know what you're talking about.

EDITH. We're scared – both of us.

MAE ELLEN. Everybody's scared about Charlie –

EDITH. And you're scared about me leaving the church. About your organ being destroyed – wondering if it'll be replaced – who the new pastor will be – how you'll fit in –

MAE ELLEN. I'll be just fine.

EDITH. I know you will. I'm just worried about what *you think.*

MAE ELLEN. *(with a touch of anger)* I said I'll be all right!

EDITH. You're angry at me too –

MAE ELLEN. I'm not angry at anybody.

EDITH. If it helps, I know I should've told you Charlie was retiring the minute I knew.

MAE ELLEN. I guessed. Okay?

> *(***EDITH*** *smiles at* **MAE ELLEN** *and the two women look at one another.)*

EDITH. When he told me, Mae Ellen, one thing popped into my head. It had nothing to do with going on a cruise or being free of committee meetings and holier-than-thou people who think they're on the inside track to Heaven. It was, oh, Lord, if this means I'll have to leave Mae Ellen, how can I go with him? You, sweetie, have been a huge part of my life since you first walked though that church door thirty years ago telling me you could play an organ.

MAE ELLEN. I was right, wasn't I?

EDITH. Oh, you own that thing, and always have. Too bad your idea of what should be played at a Baptist worship service was...well, pretty much *your* idea.

MAE ELLEN. I'm still around.

EDITH. And First Baptist of Ivy Gap is better because you are.

MAE ELLEN. Of course...if it *hadn't* been for you –

EDITH. Hey, Charlie and I love surprises. Especially on Sunday mornings.

MAE ELLEN. Maybe I *would've* moved on –

EDITH. I believe we'd had this conversation, Mae Ellen.

MAE ELLEN. I might've gone somewhere where I would've –

EDITH. Where you would've become a big famous music star.

MAE ELLEN. I had dreams –

EDITH. I know you did.

MAE ELLEN. Who knows...if you've got a little talent –

EDITH. God gave you more than a little talent –

MAE ELLEN. No telling what can happen.

EDITH. In which case, I officially apologize for keeping you from being rich and famous.

MAE ELLEN. That's not what I'm saying, Edith.

EDITH. I know it isn't.

MAE ELLEN. My head...it's always been full of silly dreams –

EDITH. They weren't silly, Mae Ellen.

MAE ELLEN. None of them were going to happen, Edith! Not when you're afraid of your own shadow and always have been. And now, what I've got...things I've grown comfortable with – my job, you and Charlie, the church...they're disappearing before my eyes. And there's nothing to replace them. I end up thinking about everything. And you're right...it scares the day-lights out of me.

(**EDITH** *takes* **MAE ELLEN** *hand. After a second we hear the hospital's public address announcer.*)

ANNOUNCER. *(offstage)* Edith Ellington...room 127 please.

EDITH. *(Rises. We sense her concern.)* Go home now. We'll talk about this later.

MAE ELLEN. I'll be here. I want to hear the good news about Charlie...

(*An anxious* **EDITH** *looks at* **MAE ELLEN**, *forcing an appreciative smile. She turns and exits. At the same moment, the light on* **MAE ELLEN** *– who continues to sit – dims a bit; a second light comes up downstage left. It is* **LUCILLE**'s *home across town; there we see* **ANNIE** *sitting at small table, a pen in hand. After another moment,* **LUCILLE** *enters; she carries a tray on which there's a pot of tea and a couple of cups.*)

LUCILLE. I thought you might like a cup of tea.

ANNIE. Thank you.

LUCILLE. May I pour you a cup?

ANNIE. I'll help myself in a minute. Thank you.

> (*Silence as* LUCILLE *pours a cup of tea for herself and* ANNIE *continues writing.*)

LUCILLE. You're writing David I suppose.

> (ANNIE *nods as* LUCILLE *sits.*)

> Tell him hello for me please.

ANNIE. I will.

LUCILLE. Tell him I…wish his wife and his mama were getting along better.

ANNIE. Mrs. Spears…

LUCILLE. I've tried to make you part of things here ..

ANNIE. You have.

LUCILLE. You always seem so…

ANNIE. Pre-occupied? I know – I'm sorry.

LUCILLE. I keep telling myself you're a long way from home –

ANNIE. That's not an excuse.

LUCILLE. And you're here only because David insisted –

ANNIE. And I understood. He wants us to live here – in Ivy Gap – when he finally gets home from…(*doesn't say the word*)

LUCILLE. You can hardly say it, can you?

ANNIE. I can say it, Mrs. Spears. Vietnam.

LUCILLE. Where he is bravely serving his country.

ANNIE. He was drafted. He doesn't like it any better than I do.

LUCILLE. He is serving his country – !

ANNIE. Did you hear the news this morning? They're saying President Nixon is about to expand the war –

LUCILLE. David is serving his country! Like his father and his grandfather before him served their country!

ANNIE. (*backing off to avoid an argument*) Yes, ma'am.

LUCILLE. What don't you understand about that?

ANNIE. I'll tell David you're proud of him. *(smiles, resumes her letter writing)*

LUCILLE. Please answer my question.

ANNIE. *(after a moment)* It's...

LUCILLE. Go on...

ANNIE. It's... *this* war, Mrs. Spears –

LUCILLE. *(critically)* Oh, we don't get to choose the wars we fight, young lady.

ANNIE. Yes, ma'am. *(looking directly at **LUCILLE**, bravely)* But maybe we should.

*(**ANNIE** smiles at **LUCILLE** who turns away. As she does, lights on them dim some while the lights across the stage come up again on **MAE ELLEN** who continues to sit. After a moment, **EDITH** enters. **MAE ELLEN** sees her and rises.)*

EDITH. *(quite obvious trying to make the best of the situation)* The burns...they're healing faster than the doctors expected. Now, that's good news, huh?

MAE ELLEN. And his lungs? The smoke, and all that...?

EDITH. *That*...I'm afraid is... *(pause, bravely)* I'm afraid it's taking a little longer to fix.

MAE ELLEN. So...Edith...that means...what?

(silence)

Edith...?

EDITH. I believe it means we're going to have to pray a little harder.

*(Lights on **EDITH** and **MAE ELLEN** dim to the level on **LUCILLE** and **ANNIE**. The four women – although on separate sides of the stage – share a mutual appearance of fear. After a moment, all lights dim slowly to black.)*

End of Scene

Scene V

(It's a week or so later. The church's fellowship hall again. For the first time, we're hearing construction sounds [hammering, sawing, etc.] coming from the area that was once the sanctuary.)

*(At rise, **OLENE** is alone. After a moment, she spots a choir robe draped on a chair. She scans the hall to make sure she's alone, then crosses to the robe, slips it on, steps to the stage. Unable to resist, she proceeds to do a little strip tease while humming an appropriate song...something between what one might see in Las Vegas and that which might be permitted in a church a lot more liberal than First Baptist of Ivy Gap. As she moves across the stage, teasing a make-believe audience, she playfully removes the robe just as **ANNIE**, **LUCILLE** and **VERA** – a brown grocery sack brimming with items in her arms and sporting another colorful hat – enter. **LUCILLE** and **VERA** watch in horror as **OLENE** continues to do her thing. When she's finished, **ANNIE** applauds, that is until she notes **LUCILLE**'s scorn and realizes her mistake.)*

LUCILLE. *(hands on her hips, exasperated over **OLENE**'s performance and **ANNIE**'s approval of it.)* Never...in all my years have I seen something...so...so...*(flustered, unable to find the right words to express her disapproval)*

VERA. Lucille, please...I'll handle this. *(after a moment, placing her sack of groceries on a table, non-judgmental)* There was a time, Olene, I would've been hysterical witnessing the infamous Madam Midnight performing her routine in my church. Since then, however, I've traveled the world. I've seen things I couldn't have imagined in my wildest dreams. And now Harry – against my wishes I assure you – sneaks peeks at magazines featuring half-clothed women in degrading poses. *Which – so help me, Lucille! – shall never be repeated to another living, breathing Baptist.* *(turning back to **OLENE**, sweetly again)* Plus, I've told myself a thousand times, "Vera, you must be less judgmental, more Christian to those who say and do things that disappoint you." So...unlike somebody we know, I'll refrain from expressing my full disapproval and merely say... *"What in the H-E-double-L are you doing in my church?"*

(**OLENE** – *to* **LUCILLE'***s horror – performs one final gyration as* **MAE ELLEN** *enters. She's dressed more smartly, plus there's a bounce in her step and a twinkle in her eye we haven't seen before.*)

MAE ELLEN. Good morning...

VERA. And you, Mae Ellen! Unless my eyes are failing me – like everything else God blessed me with eons ago – you were flirting...in public no less...with one of those workers rebuilding our sanctuary.

MAE ELLEN. *(playfully)* I don't know, Vera...maybe ...

OLENE. She's started going out with him too. Isn't that right, Mae Ellen.?

MAE ELLEN. I don't know what you're talking about

OLENE. Reed Hennings, maybe?

(**MAE ELLEN** – *surprised and concerned that* **OLENE** *also knows her new friend – doesn't answer.*)

Oh, I've got my eyes on him too. And take it from me, Vera...he's not only good looking, he's...*(makes a gesture to indicates he's sexy as well.)*

LUCILLE. God is watching you, Olene!

VERA. Then it's the perfect time for another confession. The mere image of a man wearing a low-slung leather tool belt sends chills down my back...*(almost to herself)* among other places.

(**LUCILLE** *has heard more than enough which seems to please* **VERA.**)

OLENE. *(claps her hands, looks at* **MAE ELLEN** *who looks away)* I believe she's normal.

VERA. Getting more normal every day, I promise. Where's Edith?

MAE ELLEN. *(a tinge of anger in her voice)* She'll be here in a minute. She's coming from the hospital.

VERA. With good news...please, Lord.

LUCILLE. *(after a moment, looking at* **VERA** *and* **OLENE**) Now... if the two of you are through entertaining the devil, I have things I need to say.

VERA. Hold your horses till Edith gets here. *(crossing to her bags of groceries)* While we wait, I've got something important to share with Annie...who hasn't had the pleasure of meeting my Harry...who just happens, my dear, to be the reigning commander-in-chief of our church's...*(becoming increasingly critically)* illustrious board of deacons.

ANNIE. I'm looking forward to meeting him, Mrs. Reynolds.

VERA. However, you know other men, I would think.

ANNIE. Well, yes, ma'am. I'm married.

VERA. Therefore, you're aware that all of God's creatures who zip their pants in the morning think their extra extremity puts them one up on us...

LUCILLE. *(sarcastically)* Now that is truly something to share.

ANNIE. If you say so, Mrs. Reynolds.

VERA. Men – in their infinite wisdom – believe they are the crowning art of God's creation. We poor souls, on the other hand, are delegated by God and by them to perform the "lesser" duties in life...like keeping our homes sparkling, caring for our children and, above all...doing the weekly grocery shopping. Do you have any idea why that is?

OLENE. Here comes the sermon, Annie ...

VERA. Because they are plainly and utterly incapable of doing any of it! A case in point...Yesterday Harry tells me he's tired of the same old Southern suppers, those tried and true dishes that have nourished our souls for generations. If I would simply give him directions to the nearest Piggly-Wiggly, he'd venture into it on his own. Can you imagine? By his lonesome. Naturally, I said, "Thataway, Harry!" *(first pointing out the door, then to the grocery bag on the table)* This, Annie, is one of the seven sacks he returned with half a day later. The remaining six containing similar items which will, quote-unquote…"improve our dining forever". *(removes a bag from the sack, holds it up for all to see)* Among Harry's inspired selections were these… PORK RINDS! One of a dozen varieties that attracted his attention. Barbecued, salted, roasted, toasted, frosted…they fried 'em, he bought 'em. *(now removing a box from the bag)* TV DINNERS! A perfectly dazzling collection of treasured family recipes, all beautifully boxed in colorful cardboard. I cannot wait to sit down at our next Sunday dinner – Mozart playing, silver glistening, our best china staring us in the face – and the two of us – after a perfectly lovely Baptist blessing – peeling back gaudy covers reading…LIVER AND ONIONS. *(removing another box from the bag, holding it up)* And for dessert…ah, Harry's piece de resistance… MINCEMEAT SHORTCAKE! Consisting of several of my all-time favorite Southern delicacies…*(now reading from the label)* CHOPPED BEEF SUET SERVED OVER SPONGE CAKE.

ANNIE. That's funny, Mrs. Reynolds.

VERA. What isn't funny, is what isn't in these sacks… no milk, no eggs, no bread and certainly no…toilet paper. *(beat, becoming increasingly angry, perhaps throwing the packages back into the sack)* It isn't funny either that I'm an intelligent woman. Oh, I am, Olene, no matter what you think. Yet, the people in power in this world – in this church too – want me to believe the only things I'm capable of doing are those they don't want to do. Or in Harry's case…can't do.

ANNIE. You can't fool me, Mrs. Reynolds. I know you love him.

VERA. I love my cocker spaniel too. That doesn't mean I have to cook him three meals a day, then let him whisper sweet nothings in my ear.

LUCILLE. Why are you are so hard on that man?

VERA. Don't mess with me, Lucille. You cannot win.

LUCILLE. I assure you, Annie, Harry Reynolds is a good Christian and a fine gentleman.

VERA. A good Christian maybe. But a fine gentleman lowers the toilet seat. *(shaking her head, raising her hands, exasperated)* Ignore me, Annie…I'll feel better this afternoon. I'm shopping. And if the shoe fits, I'm buying a pair in every color and charging Harry.

LUCILLE. *(to* **VERA**, *angrily)* With or without Edith, I have far more important things to discuss than your problems with men!

VERA. Name one.

LUCILLE. This…*(She can barely bring herself to say the word.)*…show! This work of the devil!

VERA. Oh, I hardly think –

LUCILLE. The Bible warns us that "we must stand firm against the schemes of the devil".

OLENE. *(chuckling at the thought of it)* Schemes of the devil…?

LUCILLE. "For our struggle is not against flesh and blood, but against the spiritual forces of wickedness in heavenly places." Ephesians…six, eleven.

*(*OLENE *now laughs openly at* LUCILLE*'s words.)*

Laugh all you want, Olene! Just remember, if I have a vote on this…and the talent –

VERA. *(looks disapprovingly at* OLENE*)* Such as it is –

LUCILLE. Isn't appropriate for a Baptist Church. None of this will see the light of day—so help me! *(to* **VERA***)* Obviously, the deacon board will have to approve everything –

VERA. I believe we can do without getting men involved –

LUCILLE. Without the deacon board's approval, there will be none of this. Period!

ANNIE. Actually, I've done some thinking about everything. *(realizing* **LUCILLE** *will disapprove)* But, then, you're the only people in the church I know. So I'll just keep my mouth shut –

OLENE. As Edith would say, speak up!

ANNIE. Okay, I will. The first thing I think we should do is pick a theme –

LUCILLE. None of this is wise, Annie.

ANNIE. Yes, ma'am. *(ignoring* **LUCILLE***)* For example, "Showtime at First Baptist".

LUCILLE. God help us…

OLENE. "Showtime"…I love it.

ANNIE. We'll need a piano—

VERA. My contribution…with conditions, of course.

ANNIE. And a master of ceremonies to introduce people, acts. Olene, maybe that could be you—

OLENE. I don't know about that…*(wouldn't want it any other way)* However, if you insist.

ANNIE. We'll probably want to hold auditions—

LUCILLE. *(critically)*	**OLENE.** *(enthusiastically)*
Just like Hollywood.	Just like Hollywood!

ANNIE. I have notes in the car…promotion suggestions, ticket pricing ideas…if anybody's interested…

OLENE. You bet we are, Annie.

ANNIE. All right then. I'll be right back.

> *(Excitedly,* **ANNIE** *crosses to the door; as she does,* **OLENE** *looks at her as she sings the following to the tune of* "Give Me That Old-Time Religion," *making up the words as she sings.)*

OLENE.

> "Give us that…SHOW-time religion."

> *(Although still troubled and withdrawn,* **MAE ELLEN** *manages to clap along with* **OLENE***'s singing.)*

> "We want that SHOW-time religion.

> It's just like OLD-time religion,

> And it's good enough for us."

> *(As* **ANNIE** *exits,* **LUCILLE** *glares at* **OLENE***; she's horrified.)*

LUCILLE. Olene Wiffer! Either Las Vegas has completely rotted your brain! Or you've totally forgotten where you are! Which I doubt!

VERA. Lucille, relax.

LUCILLE. Relax? When everything I believe is being assaulted? Oh, I don't think so!

VERA. It's a hymn...*(begins to sing)* "Give me that –

LUCILLE. *(interrupting, highly emotional)* – "SHOW-TIME religion...it's just like OLD-TIME religion." Well, it's not good enough for me. And it shouldn't be for any of us, especially you, Vera!

VERA. I believe you're going to have a heart attack.

LUCILLE. I cannot tell you how I've prayed about this. And the Lord – like always – answered my prayer...in a way that made me sit up and pay attention.

OLENE. This I want to hear ...

LUCILLE. Let our guard down – allow this ungodly thing to go on – what's next? Dancing in the aisles? Toasting Him with hard drink? Carrying on like...well, like big-city, wine-sipping Episcopalians?

OLENE. God told you that.

LUCILLE. Ephesians tells me, "Do not give the devil an opportunity". God told me this show of yours is like... KUDZU!

OLENE. KUDZU! *(claps, greatly amused by LUCILLE's analogy)*

LUCILLE. Which also started out as a "good idea". But, let your guard down...let one of those little devil seeds flutter into the wind.

OLENE. *(continuing to make fun of LUCILLE's hyperbole, laughing)* Devil seeds now—

(ANNIE *re-enters as* LUCILLE *carries on. Her solemn demeanor – she looks as if she's seen a ghost – catches everybody's but* LUCILLE's *attention.*)

LUCILLE. Before you can say, "Hide the kids, Nelly," the world is veiled...in that vicious little vine that ate the South!

ANNIE. I just ran into your husband, Mrs. Reynolds.

VERA. In the parking lot?

ANNIE. Yes, ma'am. He asked me to give you all a message.

(silence as all look at **ANNIE** *in anxious anticipation)*

He said...he thinks you should...*(understanding the seriousness of what she's about to announce)* He thinks all of you should meet him at the hospital as soon as possible.

MAE ELLEN, VERA & OLENE. Charlie...!

LUCILLE.	**VERA.**
Oh, Lord...	NO...

(There's a collective gasp as the women look at one another in horror. After a moment, **MAE ELLEN, VERA, LUCILLE** *and* **OLENE** *dash out of the hall.* **ANNIE** *remains, as lights slowly dim to black.)*

End of Act I

ACT II

Scene I

(The church's fellowship hall, four days later, late morning. Tables in the hall are now covered with white table cloths, and a small potted plant sits in the center of each. Also, a few coffee cups, plates, etc., remain on the tables, suggesting the space was recently the scene of a reception. An upright piano [or keyboard] covered with a cloth, now sits against a back wall.)

*(At rise, **VERA** and **MAE ELLEN** are doing the final clearing of the tables. Attired in dark dresses covered with plain white aprons, they work in silence for a long moment. **VERA** wears a conservative black hat.)*

VERA. Except for men – who I'm beginning to think even God can't fix – I'm not overly critical. Tell me that's true, Mae Ellen...

*(A sad **MAE ELLEN** goes about her business without responding.)*

I'm asking because I just had a run-in with that busybody, Helen Sue Randle, bless her heart. I'm sitting there – my head is bowed, my Bible is in my hand – quietly telling Harry his shoes don't match. Who slides next to me, but the gossip queen of Ivy Gap. Before God could seal her lips, she's telling me in glowing detail – in church, no less – that half of Ivy Gap is playing house with the other half...in the process naming names. Fortunately, I know what the Bible *really* says about loving thy neighbor. So I tell her – with a smile in my voice – I'm hearing things too from a *very* reliable source...that unless she shuts down her imagination and closes her mouth *(with a smile in her voice)*...she'll be spending eternity where the sun don't shine. Can you imagine, Mae Ellen? What our Holy Bible would look like if Helen Sue Randle had written it? There is one saving grace, of course...she *is* a Presbyterian.

(VERA and MAE ELLEN lapse into thoughtful silence. After a moment, VERA senses MAE ELLEN is on the verge of tears.)

VERA. Oh, Mae Ellen. I know how you feel. That's why I keep reminding myself...

(LUCILLE enters, followed by OLENE. Both wear dark dresses, although OLENE's is a tad less conservative. They remove their aprons as they enter.)

If anybody's going to Heaven –

OLENE. *(She overheard VERA's comment as she entered.)* *If* there *is* a Heaven, of course.

MAE ELLEN. Olene! Not now!

LUCILLE. For someone who doesn't believe in God, you certainly spend a lot of time at church.

OLENE. I didn't say I don't believe in God!

LUCILLE. Well, you could've fooled me, Olene!

MAE ELLEN. *Stop it – !*

LUCILLE. If I didn't know better, I'd say you've come home looking for forgiveness.

MAE ELLEN. *For God's sake, Lucille –*

LUCILLE. We know she was a stripper, Mae Ellen. It's what we don't know that may be the problem.

MAE ELLEN. DON'T YOU UNDERSTAND...! *(after a moment, suddenly aware of the finality of it all)* We just buried Charlie!

(A period of peace as the women begin clearing the remaining dishes, etc.)

I thought it was...beautiful.

VERA. It *was* beautiful, Mae Ellen.

MAE ELLEN. Every pew full.

VERA. Flowers everywhere.

MAE ELLEN. Not a dry eye in the place.

(EDITH enters without OLENE seeing her. Of course, she's also wearing a dark dress.)

OLENE. Too bad the "place" turned out to be a Methodist church. I wonder what Charlie would've said about that.

EDITH. He would've said, "Thank you" to all of our wonderful Methodist friends.

OLENE. Edith, I'm sorry –

EDITH. It's all right, Olene. I've asked myself the same question. And knowing him like I do... *(catching herself, managing to smile)* I'm going to have to work on my tenses, huh? Knowing Charlie, he would've been amused the service was in a Methodist church overflowing with card-carrying Baptists –

VERA. Presbyterians, Episcopalians –

LUCILLE. A few confused Catholics.

VERA. You name it, Edith. Everybody in Ivy Gap was there.

(EDITH nods, appearing particularly fragile at the moment.)

MAE ELLEN. Edith, sit down.

EDITH. Really, Mae Ellen. I'm doing all right. And since you've got everything here under control. There I go again...forgetting to thank y'all for everything –

OLENE. It was nothing, Edith.

EDITH. It was too...serving all those folks beautifully like you did.

VERA. We wanted to do something here, in our church.

EDITH. And it was lovely...all the casseroles, cobblers –

VERA. You know Baptists, Edith. We don't go anywhere without a covered dish.

EDITH. *(managing to smile)* Including heaven, I hear. Now... if you'll excuse me, I believe I need to get on home...

(EDITH takes a step toward the door before becoming noticeably unsteady. MAE ELLEN steps to her, takes her arm. At the same time, VERA grabs a chair and positions it behind EDITH.)

EDITH. *(sits, becoming increasingly emotional)* I've told myself a hundred times, "Be strong, Edith. Nobody wants to see an old lady cry."

MAE ELLEN. Edith, you need to talk.

EDITH. You know me. Don't you, sweetie? *(catching her breath before speaking)* I knew we were in trouble when pneumonia set in, and the doctors kept telling me things I didn't understand. Still, I never let myself believe he could die. That everything we had planned – all those wonderful things we looked forward to doing together – would go with him. Now, when I think I can't stand it anymore – in the middle of the night when I think about what I've lost, when my heart feels like it's been ripped from my chest – I remind myself he's in a better place. That makes me feel selfish. That instead of crying myself back asleep I should rejoice, praise God. That's when I get mad. I get mad at myself, and at Charlie for dying...and, worse, I get mad at God. So mad, I could spit. Then it starts all over again, and I feel lost and alone and have no idea what's going to happen and wonder if any of it makes any difference. *(wipes a tear from her eye)*

LUCILLE. "He shall wipe away every tear from their eyes; and there shall no longer be any death; there shall no longer be any mourning or crying." Revelations... chapter twenty-one, verse four.

VERA. *(looking at LUCILLE, critically)* John...chapter eleven, verse thirty-five..."Jesus *wept*."

EDITH. *(rallying)* If he were here, of course, he'd be all over me for talking like that. He'd say, "Edith, I'm just a little ahead of you here. You'll carry on...do God's work while you can...make me proud of you. Some day, not so very long from now, we'll be together again. And I promise...it'll be better than any retirement could ever be."

VERA. That sounds like Charlie.

EDITH. *(repeating words much as Charlie might have said them)* "Come work for the Lord. The hours are long, the work is hard, but the retirement benefits...oh, they are out of this world!"

VERA. He said that a thousand times.

EDITH. He had a wonderful sense of humor.

VERA. Many a Sunday, I laughed more than I prayed.

MAE ELLEN. Remember the sermon, Edith…"Ten Ways To Tell She's A Preacher's Wife?"

EDITH. Of course, I do, Mae Ellen. He gave it on our twenty-fifth wedding anniversary.

MAE ELLEN. Number five…"She keeps her words both soft and tender because tomorrow she may have to eat them."

VERA. Number one's a whole lot better. Right too, if you ask me… *(looks at* **EDITH** *with admiration)* "She opens her mouth in wisdom, and teaching of kindness is on her tongue." Except the man stole it, Edith! From Proverbs.

EDITH. This morning…sitting there…tears in my eyes…I kept remembering the wonderful things Charlie gave me through the years. The big one I decided – the one that changed my life, made it extra special – was being a part of his church. Without it I'd be missing what's most important to me now…my wonderful First Baptist family. Especially all of you. Talk about a gift, huh?

(Tears well in **EDITH***'s eyes;* **MAE ELLEN** *steps to her.)*

No, no. I'm going to have to learn to do this by myself. Along with a little help from my friends. *(She stands.)*

(Whether she needs it or not, **MAE ELLEN**, **VERA**, **OLENE**, *and* **LUCILLE** *give* **EDITH** *a community hug.)*

See…you're all a girl needs. Thank you. *(smiles, steps toward the door)*

OLENE. Edith *(hesitates)*…

EDITH. You have something you want to say, Olene?

OLENE. A question. But this isn't the time –

EDITH. Oh, I know you too, Olene. You want to know about the talent show. Whether you should plan to go ahead with it.

LUCILLE. The answer is obvious, Edith. The show is off.

EDITH. That's what you think Charlie would want?

LUCILLE. And what you should want as well. I mean, we've lost our sanctuary and now we've buried our *(hesitates)*...

EDITH. Our pastor. You can say it, Lucille.

LUCILLE. I know what you keep saying about raising money and spirits. That's a noble thought. But this is hardly the time –

EDITH. Does it matter Charlie loved the idea?

LUCILLE. Why we're even discussing it, I don't understand. God and the deacon board will have none of it.

VERA. As far as the board goes, I might have something to say about that. Depending on what you think, Edith.

(Silence as all look at **EDITH.** *)*

EDITH. What I think?

LUCILLE. Edith, please. At a time like this, nobody needs to *(hesitating)*...

EDITH. Smile or laugh. Or feel good about anything. Is that what you were about to say, Lucille?

OLENE. Edith. What do we do?

(Silence as once again all look at **EDITH.** *)*

EDITH. I believe I remember Mae Ellen came up with a clever name for our little planning group here.

LUCILLE. Edith! Listen to me! This is the wrong time for a bad idea!

EDITH. Mae Ellen, would you please remind Lucille and the rest of us what that name was?

MAE ELLEN. *(looking at* **OLENE,** *obviously preferring not to be a part of the process)* I don't know that I remember, Edith.

OLENE. Well, I sure do.

EDITH. All right...

OLENE. It was...*(with a smile in her voice)* it was...Charlie's Angels.

*(***EDITH** *looks at* **LUCILLE** *and the others, all of whom know* **EDITH** *has answered* **OLENE**'s *question.)*

OLENE. *(looking to the heavens, softly to herself)* Thank you, Charlie!

(BLACKOUT)

End of Scene

Scene II

(The fellowship hall, a month or so later. The table cloths, potted plants, etc., are gone as is the cloth that draped the piano in the previous scene. Also missing is the lectern, replaced by a microphone on a stand.)

(At rise, we again hear occasional construction sounds. Meanwhile, **MAE ELLEN** *sits at the piano facing the audience; she plays something that one might hear at the opening of a Las Vegas act, although her performance lacks enthusiasm. As she plays, she looks at* **OLENE** *who stands behind the mike. If a glance could kill,* **OLENE** *would be dead.* **ANNIE** *sits in what looks a bit like a director's chair and watches* **OLENE**. **ANNIE** *wears a raincoat; a pad of paper rests on her lap.)*

OLENE. *(enthusiastically as the up tempo music continues)* Ladies and gentlemen. Welcome to the fabulous Riviera Hotel on Las Vegas' glittering neon strip –

ANNIE. Olene…!

OLENE. Tonight we present a dazzling collection of –

ANNIE. *It won't fly, Olene!* It's…

(As **ANNIE** *shakes her head,* **MAE ELLEN** *'s piano playing comes to an unceremonious end.)*

OLENE. *It's* nowhere close, is it?

ANNIE. Maybe you want to try something a little more like…well, like Ivy Gap.

OLENE. Something like this you mean…

*(***OLENE** *nods at* **MAE ELLEN** *who, although obviously unhappy with* **OLENE**, *understands the message and proceeds to play something somber that one would not hear in Las Vegas.* **OLENE** *'s lack of enthusiasm matches the music.)*

Welcome, ladies and gentlemen, to *totally* amateur night at a small-minded Baptist church in Stick-Your-Head-In-The-Sand, Tennessee.

(Once again, with a bang of the keys, MAE ELLEN stops playing.)

ANNIE. What ever happened to "Showtime at First Baptist"?

OLENE. Somebody'll object to that too. Her name is Lucille.

ANNIE. Maybe I can work on her.

OLENE. In that case…Maestro…

(OLENE looks at MAE ELLEN who looks away; it's increasingly obvious that OLENE is the cause of MAE ELLEN's current unhappiness.)

Mae Ellen…!

(A reluctant MAE ELLEN knows what OLENE wants and now proceeds to play it; it is something between the two previous pieces.)

Ladies and gentlemen, it's time to turn down the lights and turn up your expectations. Because – ready or not – it's…*Showtime at First Baptist…*

(ANNIE stands, cheers, claps, then – a tad embarrassed – sits.)

A fantastic evening of fabulous entertainment, showcasing the hidden talents of people you know and love. So, sit back, get ready to smile…to laugh once again. *Because here they are…(stops in mid-sentence, looks to her audience)* Whatdaya think?

ANNIE. I think it's good. Don't you, Mae Ellen?

MAE ELLEN. *(stops playing, speaks cynically to ANNIE)* Read me your list of "fabulous" entertainment. Tell me about all this "talent" hiding in our pews on Sunday mornings…

ANNIE. We have a juggler who tosses hymnals…

MAE ELLEN. *(not impressed)* Really?

ANNIE. And a beagle…supposedly she sings and dances –

MAE ELLEN. Let me guess…her name's Amazing Grace, and she does the dog-trot.

ANNIE. Somebody who recites the books of the Bible –

MAE ELLEN. My mama could do that.

ANNIE. Backwards…in order…while standing on her head? *(pause)* Also a gospel trio –

MAE ELLEN. The fabulous tin-eared Birdie Sisters who'll –

OLENE. You sound like you're mad at the world, Mae Ellen.

MAE ELLEN. Who'll chirp like angels in paradise.

ANNIE. And lots more. Some of them have to be…*semi*-fabulous. Don't they?

MAE ELLEN. None of them would see the light of day.

OLENE. You don't know, Mae Ellen.

MAE ELLEN. I know Lucille's meeting with the deacon board this morning –

OLENE. With Vera. Who'll be here in a minute.

MAE ELLEN. And I know Lucille isn't going to stop till she has her way. So rehearse all you want. Get Elvis Presley to join in. It isn't going to happen.

(**MAE ELLEN** *closes the piano lid, stands as a triumphant* **VERA** *marches into the hall wearing another in her wardrobe of hates. She takes a second look at* **ANNIE**'s *raincoat, but says nothing.* **ANNIE**, **MAE ELLEN**, *and* **OLENE** *look at her in anticipation.*)

VERA. I have had the most interesting morning!

OLENE. Just tell us what the board decided.

VERA. And miss the fun part? *(pause)* There I am, Olene… sitting in the holiest inner sanctum of the opposite sex. Where even angels fear to tread. Lucille is talking up a storm…getting men to do what they never do…listen. In a wink, she's made her case…this show of yours is a calculated plan of the devil and his disciples! Somebody calls for a vote…hands go up. The board cannot wait to save us all from hell and damnation. Then…from the head of the table…comes a voice of reason –

OLENE. Harry.

VERA. *Harry has seen the light!*

OLENE. Without you saying a word.

VERA. Olene, please. After forty years of marraige, I know what sparks Harry's engine. *(She smiles seductively.)* So… just as Rosie the Riveter helped win the war, I saved the show!

(VERA *accepts congrats as* ANNIE *and* OLENE *celebrate.*
MAE ELLEN *remains reserved.*)

VERA. What I didn't tell Harry, of course, was that the two
of you would be a part of it. Nor did I tell him I don't
trust either of you to bow your heads for the Lord's
Prayer. So tell me what you're planning. Maybe I won't
feel like I'm on the Titanic, surrounded by iceberg,
sharks and a ship of heathens about to call on God.

OLENE. We've got ourselves a show-stopping act.

ANNIE. I think it's pretty good, too, Mrs. Reynolds. Especially since they're letting me be a part of it.

VERA. Have you told Lucille that?

ANNIE. No, ma'am.

VERA. Then God be with you, my dear, for you are living
dangerously.

ANNIE. I think I'm thinking the same thing.

(VERA *senses that* ANNIE *is having a hard time dealing
with* LUCILLE, *not to mention Ivy Gap.*)

VERA. I was born nosey. So I've got an excuse. You're not
doing so good, are you, Annie?

ANNIE. I don't want to say anything behind anybody's back –

VERA. Hey, it's an old Southern tradition –

ANNIE. Well…I shouldn't. But if you think it's okay. The
night I met David, and he told me he was from someplace I never heard of called Ivy Gap, bells should've
gone off. I should've known we were from two really
different worlds. Especially when I couldn't understand half of what he was saying.

VERA. The boy does have a drippy drawl.

ANNIE. My poor mama – she hasn't understood a word
he's said. In spite of that and everything else, we fell in
love. When he asked me to marry him – oh, I understood that just fine! – I considered myself the luckiest
girl in the whole world. I still do. Then, before the
wedding, I visited down here. Everything seemed so…
well, it seemed so normal –

VERA. We were on our very best behavior.

ANNIE. Oh, I believe that, Mrs. Reynolds. Because everybody I met was wonderful. The town turned out to be prettier than I had imagined. His parents – they were as nice as I had hoped –

VERA. Then...

ANNIE. After the wedding, we learned David had been drafted. We talked about it, and we agreed I'd live here, with Mr. and Mrs. Spears. I'd find a good job. Which isn't going to happen...not when you have a minor in theatre and a major in international business. In time, David would come home. He'd go to work in Mr. Spears' automobile business. We'd live happily ever after.

VERA. In Ivy Gap...

ANNIE. That was the plan. Yes, ma'am.

VERA. And now...?

ANNIE. This is the part that's going to sound awful. Things are different down here, Mrs. Reynolds. I mean, where else in the universe would I be chauffeured around in a bright red Cadillac with a siren blaring, lights blinking, half scaring people off the road? Or wake up in the morning and go to bed at night, hearing Bible verses ringing in my ears. I swear – which *I know* I can't do down here – Mrs. Spears knows the Bible better than you, Mrs. Ellington, and the Pope...*combined.* Little things, too...like grits and okra and butter beans staring up at me from my dinner plate. Learning that the entire South has three spices...salt, pepper and barbecue sauce. Discovering that when people talk religion here, they're including hunting and football. So many things are...well, different, strange to me... and I guess I'm not dealing with any of them like I should. And it's my fault – I know that. Just like I know I shouldn't have opened my mouth about any of this.

VERA. However, you feel better.

ANNIE. Uh-huh. But I'd die if Mrs. Spears knew any of what I've said.

VERA. Why would we tell her? We love knowing something she doesn't know.

ANNIE. Then maybe you'd like to know something else…

(ANNIE meekly removes her raincoat, revealing a waitress's outfit from the fifties, perhaps something very pink that "Flo, the Waitress" might have worn.)

(Showing off the costume while attempting a Southern accent, not very happy about either.) Now, y'all ready for more sweet tea?

VERA. The Dixie Dew Diner.

ANNIE. Uh-huh.

VERA. And Lucille doesn't know.

ANNIE. Uh-uh.

VERA. Oh, I do hope the tips are good.

ANNIE. I had to do something, Mrs. Reynolds. *(hurriedly puts her coat back on)*

VERA. I know you did.

OLENE. When they hired me, they promised me they served "good-old home cooking just like my mama served." Well, I don't think *my* mama ever served…*(once again falls into a strong Southern drawl)* Collard greens, cornbread, black-eyed peas, with a hunk of who-knows-what swimming in the middle. Oh, Lord. Listen to me. I'm even starting to talk like y'all.

VERA. Part of the plan, Annie. We get you breathing our fresh air, eating our down-home cooking. Before you know it, you're talking like us. *(pauses, sympathetically)* Hey, there are far worse things in this world. Come here…let me give you a big Southern hug.

(VERA smiles at ANNIE, who steps to her. They hug, after which VERA turns to OLENE and MAE ELLEN.)

I'm trusting the two of you not to embarrass yourself. Or our church. Or Charlie's memory. I've said what I came to say. Now, I'm off to the country club to hold Harry's hand.

ANNIE. Is something wrong?

VERA. You haven't heard?

ANNIE. I don't think so.

VERA. Well, the news is all over town. The club's board of trustees voted last night – in its infinite wisdom – to grant women morning tee-times. Bless their charitable hearts, we – the members of the not-to-be-taken seriously society – will finally be allowed to chase that silly white ball in the cool of the day. As far as Harry's concerned…America might as well have elected a woman president. *(gleefully)* The man will never be the same.

ANNIE. What are you going to do, Mrs. Reynolds?

VERA. Whatdaya think? I'm signing up for golf lessons. After which I'm dropping by Edith's house. It's time Edith starts being Edith again. Annie, I've got a big job for you –

ANNIE. Yes, ma'am…

VERA. Watch over these clever ladies for me, okay? There's no telling the trouble they could get you in.

ANNIE. I won't let them do anything you wouldn't do, Mrs. Reynolds.

VERA. *(facetiously)* Now, that is comforting.

(VERA smiles at ANNIE, then takes her hand as a supportive gesture. As VERA crosses to the door, MAE ELLEN – still fuming – plays appropriate "walking" music on the piano. VERA – who walks to the music in an exaggerated fashion – looks back as she opens the door; it's obvious she isn't a bit happy at MAE ELLEN's contribution to her exit. The moment VERA is gone, the music stops with a crashing sound.)

OLENE. All right, Mae Ellen. What's wrong?

MAE ELLEN. *(snaps at OLENE)* What do you think is wrong?

OLENE. We have no idea. Do we, Annie?

ANNIE. Don't put me in the middle of this, Olene. I am off to my exciting new career…greens and grits, here I come. *(turns, is about to take a step toward the door, stops)* And don't you dare play that thing, Mae Ellen.

(ANNIE cautiously crosses to the door, looking back at

MAE ELLEN *as she does. She opens the door and exits.)*

OLENE. You're upset about losing the organ – all the changes going on. They worry you – I understand that, Mae Ellen. Then Charlie dies…it was unexpected and awful, and we're all sick about it. And now a new pastor's about to be called, and nobody knows anything about him, and you don't know how you'll fit in. But why take it out on me? Have *I* done something? *(silence)* Talk to me, Mae Ellen!

*(***MAE ELLEN** *turns and slowly crosses to the door. She doesn't look back, nor does she close the door after her exit. We hear more construction sounds.* **OLENE** *– believing the door was left open intentionally – steps to it, looks out.)*

Oh, Lord! Is *that* what this is all about?

*(***OLENE** *continues to look out the door. At she does the lights dim, and we begin to hear music from the 1960s, a folk song perhaps.)*

End of Scene

Scene III

(Initially, LUCILLE*'s home, the following afternoon, another setting created [in this case, downstage left] by sound and lighting, a chair or two and a small radio that sits on a table. The music we've heard through the scene change plays on that radio.)*

(At rise, we see LUCILLE *and* ANNIE, *who is seated. She reads a newspaper as she listens to the music.* LUCILLE *stands along side; she looks out without speaking. After a long moment,* ANNIE *looks at* LUCILLE, *then turns off the radio.)*

LUCILLE. Thank you.

ANNIE. I should know you don't care for that music.

LUCILLE. I've decided, if it's important to you –

ANNIE. It isn't, really. *(smiles, then returns to reading her newspaper; after a long moment, looks up, cautiously)* There's something – a couple of things...I should mention –

LUCILLE. Oh...?

ANNIE. *(gingerly)* You know, of course, I've gotten a kick out of the church's talent show –

LUCILLE. I cannot tell you, Annie, how I hate that word.

ANNIE. It's not exactly a "show" –

LUCILLE. And frankly, it displeases me that you've become involved in the planning. David would be disappointed –

ANNIE. I've written him. He thinks it's a terrific idea.

LUCILLE. I cannot imagine that's true.

ANNIE. I'll show you his letter –

LUCILLE. So you know, Annie...I have another meeting with the board of deacons this afternoon. We'll resolve this once and for all. Now...you have things to tell me…

ANNIE. I was…*(hesitates, then looks down at the newspaper, smiles)* I was wondering if you saw the story about the woman who rode in the Kentucky Derby yesterday –

LUCILLE. She lost.

ANNIE. Yes, ma'am. But she was the first woman to ride in the –

LUCILLE. She came in fifteenth.

(Silence as the two women look at one another for a long moment.)

ANNIE. *(light heartedly, in an effort to change the tone of the conversation)* Guess who I've discovered loves horses?

*(**LUCILLE** looks at **ANNIE** for an answer.)*

Your son, of course.

LUCILLE. Now, that surprises me.

ANNIE. Why?

LUCILLE. It's a long story.

ANNIE. I want to know everything about him…

LUCILLE. *(after a moment)* A long time ago, David was a Boy Scout –

ANNIE. See? I didn't know that.

LUCILLE. Well, he was. And his troop rode horses. On a ride a long way from here he got separated from the others. Then something spooked his horse…it ran away –

ANNIE. Oh, my…

LUCILLE. That evening, the sheriff called. He told us the horse had wandered back, but David was missing. You hear those words…it's cold and dark outside…your mind starts thinking awful thoughts…

ANNIE. I'm sure.

LUCILLE. His daddy, of course, went looking for him. While I did what I do when things don't look so good…I fell on my knees. I begged the Lord to watch over him.

ANNIE. I'm betting your prayers were answered.

LUCILLE. That depends…

ANNIE. Oh...?

LUCILLE. I asked God to bring my boy back in one piece. I didn't ask – while I was sitting here worrying myself sick – that Wallace would find him on a farmer's porch in the middle of nowhere...not only laughing his head off, but finishing his third helping of apple pie...then claim it was better than his mama's.

    *(**ANNIE** and **LUCILLE** share a rare laugh.)*

ANNIE. I love that story, Mrs. Spears.

LUCILLE. In spite of that one misadventure, David has been a wonderful son –

ANNIE. We are so incredibly blessed. Aren't we?

LUCILLE. I'm sure that's why I worry about him like I do.

ANNIE. *(referring to his trail ride)* Well, obviously, he can take of himself.

LUCILLE. Most of all, I pray for him. I trust you do as well.

ANNIE. Sure I do.

LUCILLE. *(smiling)* Then I know he'll walk through that door just like he left.

ANNIE. I do something else, too...

LUCILLE. Oh...?

    *(**LUCILLE** looks to **ANNIE**, wanting her to continue. **ANNIE** knows she's already said too much.)*

ANNIE. It isn't important, really.

LUCILLE. If it affects David, I'd like to know...

ANNIE. It does. At least I hope it does. But only indirectly.

LUCILLE. There are few things I hate more than secrets, Annie.

ANNIE. I write letters –

LUCILLE. We both write letters.

ANNIE. I write letters to newspapers.

    *(**LUCILLE** is surprised, but doesn't say anything.)*

I write them to the New York Times...the Washington Post –

LUCILLE. I see.

ANNIE. A few even get published.

LUCILLE. Letters protesting the war...

ANNIE. Expressing my opinion about the war. Yes, ma'am.

LUCILLE. The war David is fighting. Boys are dying in.

> (**ANNIE** *nods, fearful where this conversation is going.*)

What exactly do you think your letters will accomplish?

ANNIE. I don't know if they'll accomplish anything.

LUCILLE. Nevertheless, you write them.

ANNIE. I don't think I could live with myself if I didn't.

LUCILLE. I see.

ANNIE. It's wonderful to pray for something important – I pray all the time. But I'd like to think there's something else we can do. Something...proactive –

LUCILLE. Like write letters that undermine the war and our president –

ANNIE. Read the front page of the newspaper. Four students at a college in Ohio were killed yesterday. They were protesting the president's decision to bomb Cambodia, expand the war. They thought it was wrong. That this whole terrible war is wrong –

LUCILLE. Please don't say that in my house!

ANNIE. *(after a moment, nodding her head)* Okay.

LUCILLE. Do you understand?

ANNIE. Yes, ma'am. As long as you understand we want the same thing. For David to come home...just like he came home after being lost in the woods. We're just going about trying to make it happen in different ways. Tell me you understand *that*, Mrs. Spears?

> (**LUCILLE** *and* **ANNIE** *look at one another; the sadness and fear they share is evident. After a moment, the light on them begins to dim. As it does, another comes up downstage right. It reveals – through the use of lighting, sound, a chair, perhaps a table – the porch of* **EDITH**'s *home; it's the same afternoon. A brown packing box – the top is open – rests on the table. We see* **EDITH** *as she places various items in the box. After a moment, she picks up a leather-bound Bible. Judging by the delicate*

*manner she handles it, we realize it has special mean-
ing to her. A stressed* **MAE ELLEN** *sits in the chair next
to her.)*

EDITH. I'd fuss at him, Mae Ellen. Say, "Charlie, it's time to
replace this old worn thing. *(looks at the Bible)* Let me
buy you a fancy new one. Type easier to read. Jesus'
words spelled out in big, bold red letters." He'd hear
none of it. I knew why, of course...it would've been
like saying good-bye to an old friend who had shown
him the way almost from the beginning. *(pause, as she
pages through the Bible)* Pages torn, corners turned back,
passages underlined in a rainbow of colors...I can't
imagine anybody wanting it. I suppose though if it can
inspire somebody else half as much as it inspired him
.. he'd expect me to pass it on. *(She carefully, reluctantly
places the book in the box.)*

MAE ELLEN. Edith, I asked you a question!

EDITH. And I don't know what to tell you, Mae Ellen! The
Lord knows you've been talking about it for thirty
years. "One of these days, Edith, I'm walking out that
door. I'm going to Nashville or Knoxville" or one of a
dozen other places. All of which looked more exciting
to you than Ivy Gap. Now – at the point in your life
when most people settle down – you've decided that
time has come. Well, I don't know if I can give you my
blessing. I can hardly decide what to do with Charlie's
things...and you're asking me if it's all right for you to
turn your life upside down.

MAE ELLEN. Well, my mind's made up.

EDITH. Then nothing I say will make any difference. Is that
right?

MAE ELLEN. I'll live with my sister until I find my own place.

EDITH. And a job.

MAE ELLEN. Edith, I know what I'm doing!

EDITH. Good. Because I'm not near as sure as you are.
Have you told Olene?

MAE ELLEN. No!

EDITH. The board of deacons?

MAE ELLEN. I've written a letter.

EDITH. Have you given it to them?

MAE ELLEN. Don't baby me, Edith.

EDITH. I'm not babying you, sweetie. I'm just trying to make sure you've thought this thing through.

(silence as the two women look at one another)

A night doesn't go by – not one, Mae Ellen – that I don't pray for you. Ask God to keep you well, help you find whatever it is you've been looking for all these years. Maybe He's answered that prayer, and I don't know it. Maybe leaving Ivy Gap and all the folks who love you to tears will bring you the satisfaction that's missing in your life. Tell me that's the case. Give me a reason to believe you're not running away from something. Tell me you're sure the things you want so desperately are waiting just over that mountain.

MAE ELLEN. What do I have here? There's your answer, Edith.

EDITH. You have what I have, Mae Ellen. Dear friends who love us and care if we get up in the morning. A church where we find comfort and peace and a smiling face. A pretty town made up of good folks – Baptist and otherwise – who open their arms and their hearts when we need help. Oh, we are *so* incredibly blessed, sweetie. *(pause)* Now, I'm waiting, Mae Ellen…tell me you believe giving up all that is worth the risk. Give me the word, and I'll help you pack your things, kiss you on your cheek, and send you on your way.

MAE ELLEN. It's what I don't have, Edith…

EDITH. You have what's important, Mae Ellen. You just don't seem to know it.

MAE ELLEN. Love…is that too much to expect?

EDITH. What are you talking about? I love you like the child I never had.

MAE ELLEN. I'm talking about someone to come home to…

to share my life with. I'm fifty years old, Edith. I'm
tired of being alone.

EDITH. Then do something about it. But do it here, in Ivy
Gap.

MAE ELLEN. Oh, I thought I had.

EDITH. If you're talking about Lloyd Baxter at the picnic
or –

MAE ELLEN. I'm talking about...*(pause, then bravely)* I'm
taking about Reed Hennings – that's who I'm talking
about!

EDITH. I have no idea who that is.

MAE ELLEN. Then I'll introduce you. Which won't be hard
since he's helping rebuild the church. He's a carpen-
ter, Edith. A nice looking man. About my age. Never
married. A Christian. Oh, you'd approve – you would!

EDITH. What about him, Mae Ellen?

MAE ELLEN. *(becoming increasingly emotional)* Nothing important...except for the first time in a long time I thought
I was building something that would keep me from
feeling so...incredibly lonely for the rest of my life.

EDITH. How long have you known this Mr. Hennings?

MAE ELLEN. Long enough to know he was...*(She can't quite
say it.)* Long enough to know.

EDITH. Then something happened...

MAE ELLEN. Oh, it did all right! And this time I wasn't the
one who chased him off. Uh-uh. It was one of the
"dear friends" you were talking about...one of the rea-
sons, according to you, I should stay right where I am.
"He was her kind of man." Now, who do you think told
me that?

EDITH. So you just gave up?

MAE ELLEN. Nobody has to tell me when I've lost. I've been
down that road too many times.

(**EDITH** *and* **MAE ELLEN** *look at one another. After a
moment, a very emotional* **MAE ELLEN** *turns and crosses
quickly to exit.*)

EDITH. Mae Ellen...!

(**EDITH** *pursues* **MAE ELLEN** *for a step or two.*)

Mae Ellen, come back here!

(**MAE ELLEN** *is gone.* **EDITH** *looks up to heaven.*)

EDITH. Oh, Charlie...Charlie! Where are you when I need you?

(*After a moment,* **EDITH** *slowly retraces her steps. In the process she sees the packing box on the table. She takes a deep breath, then reaches into the box, removes Charlie's Bible. She looks at it for a moment, then takes it to her chest as if it were one of the treasures of her life. With sadness and concern evident, she looks in the direction* **MAE ELLEN** *exited; as she does, the lights dim slowly to black.*)

End of Scene

Scene IV

(The church's fellowship hall, a few minutes later; it is unchanged from Scene Two.)

(At rise, the hall is empty. After a moment, **VERA** *enters wearing a purple dress and a bright red hat. As she surveys the hall, her eyes note the microphone on the stage. She hums something to herself as she glances around the room, in the process, making certain she's alone. Assured, she steps to the stage and hesitantly crosses to a position behind the microphone. No doubt knowing better, she grabs the mike and proceeds to sing* "Give My Regards to Broadway!" *Her lack of talent is obvious, but that doesn't keep her from giving it the old college try.)*

VERA.

GIVE MY REGARDS TO BROADWAY...

*(***VERA*** clears her throat, and then continues, this time a tad more confidently. As she does,* **OLENE** *enters. She wears a "flapper-era" outfit...a colorful top, shorter than normal skirt, beads, perhaps even a feather protruding for her hair. Unseen by* **VERA,** **OLENE** *watches and listens.)*

REMEMBER ME TO HERALD SQUARE!...
TELL ALL THE GANG AT FORTY-SECOND STREET
THAT I'LL SOON BE THERE!

WHISPER OF HOW I'M YEARNING...
TO MINGLE WITH THE OLD TIME THRONG!...

(now, really getting into it, attetmpting high kicks across the stage.)

GIVE MY REGARDS TO OLD BROADWAY...AND SAY...
(sees **OLENE** *looking at her, wishing she could disappear)*

...I'LL BE...THERE...
(The women look at one another. Perhaps for the first time in her life, **VERA**'s *embarrassed. She looks heavenward.)*

Oh, Lord! Take me now!

OLENE. Uh-uh. The second verse first…

(As **OLENE** *speaks, she hustles to the stage. Once there,* **VERA** *sheepishly steps away from the mike;* **OLENE** *assumes her position.)*

Which I know you were about to sing…*(She sings:)* GIVE MY REGARDS TO JESUS! –

VERA. No doubt about it, Olene. We'll slither into Hell together.

OLENE. Hey, Charlie's up there, right? I'm just asking him to say "hi" to the important folks. *(picking up the song:)* GIVE MY REGARDS TO JESUS!…REMEMBER ME TO MARY, TOO –

VERA. Forgive us, dear Lord…*especially* this wayward child. And tell me please that what I'm seeing and hearing isn't part of her act.

*(***MAE ELLEN** *enters. She remains unhappy with* **OLENE.***)*

OLENE. I wasn't sure we were going to have an act. Isn't that right, Mae Ellen?

MAE ELLEN. *(She snaps.)* I told you I'd be here.

*(***EDITH** *enters moments after* **MAE ELLEN***; it's obvious she's been pursuing* **MAE ELLEN.** *Upon seeing* **OLENE***'s attire, she does a double take, but doesn't comment.)*

EDITH. Mae Ellen, don't keep walking away from me…

MAE ELLEN. *(Ignoring* **EDITH,** *crossing directly to the piano. Sits.)* All right, Olene! You want to rehearse – let's go – I'm ready!

EDITH.	**OLENE.**
Mae Ellen…!	Mae Ellen…!

*(***MAE ELLEN** *ignores both* **EDITH** *and* **OLENE** *and begins to play the opening bar of* "Alexander's Rag-time Band.")*

EDITH.	**OLENE.**
We need to talk!	We need to talk!

(Abruptly, we hear a siren. MAE ELLEN *stops playing.)*

VERA. No time for that. We're being raided...

(The siren sound gets louder to the point it's as if it were just outside the hall, at which point it stops. After a moment, LUCILLE *enters. She sees* OLENE*'s outfit and is horrified.* OLENE *whirls back at her in a semi-suggestive manner, smiling as she does.* VERA *watches, her hands on her hips.)*

LUCILLE. *(Now turning to* EDITH *and* VERA*.)* God continues to test us. And the two of you just stand there, watching this...this *blaspheme!*

VERA. Something is always bugging you big time, Lucille.

LUCILLE. What's bugging me, Vera, is your indifference to this insult to God. Look at what the girl's got on!

(Abruptly, ANNIE *enters wearing an outfit that's a match for* OLENE*'s, complete to the feather in the hair. Her appearance all but gives* LUCILLE *a heart attack.)*

ANNIE. *(equally surprised, meekly)* Mrs. Spears...

LUCILLE. Oh, Lord. I *have* lived too long.

ANNIE. I'm sorry...

LUCILLE. Not only have you been planning this thing, Annie –

ANNIE. I tried to tell you –

LUCILLE. You're obviously performing in it as well.

OLENE. Actually...she's the star of the show.

EDITH. Hush, Olene.

LUCILLE. David would be horrified!

ANNIE. That's not true.

LUCILLE. I know my son. He'd be embarrassed to tears!

EDITH. Lucille, you are way overreacting.

ANNIE. It's all right, Mrs. Ellington.

LUCILLE. I suggest you go home this minute, young lady. Change into something...respectful.

ANNIE. Yes, ma'am.

LUCILLE. And read First Timothy, chapter two, versus nine…"I want women to adorn themselves with *proper* clothing, *modestly and discreetly.*"

(ANNIE *takes a couple of steps toward the door before turning back to* LUCILLE.)

ANNIE. I'll do what you've asked me to do. But first I need to ask you something. Especially since you're the most Christian-thinking lady I know. *(pause)* You believe what I've got on…Oh, I know it's flashy. And it's not what you're used to seeing in church. And I'm sure, Mrs. Ellington, you're thinking "what's this crazy Yankee girl wearing – ?'

EDITH. I'll admit…I don't have anything quite like it in my closet.

LUCILLE. Well, *I* won't mince words, Edith…*it's an insult to God!*

ANNIE. That's what I don't understand, Mrs. Spears. How a few square yards of cloth like this – ?

LUCILLE. Edith, I could use your help here please.

(EDITH *says nothing.*)

ANNIE. How you can disapprove of it like you do. Then – knowing God and Jesus so well – support a war David knows – most of the world knows – is wrong, yet the president is making him and others fight. What makes that awful war right and this…*(pointing to her outfit)* so horribly wrong? *(silence)* Mrs. Spears, I mean no disrespect, but I really wish you'd answer me…

(*All now look at* LUCILLE *who's flustered and at a loss to explain her logic.*)

LUCILLE. The point is moot! I've met again with the deacon board. One word from me…they've cancelled the show.

VERA. Harry said "no" ?

LUCILLE. The entire board said "no." First Timothy…"I do not allow a woman to teach or exercise authority over a man, *but to remain quiet.*"

VERA. We've been neighbors more years than I care to remember, Lucille Spears. I've bitten my tongue a hundred times rather than walk next door and tell you you're a fanatic when it comes to this church and what should or should not go on here. And I promise you, I *know* a fanatic when I see one –

LUCILLE. A fanatic –

VERA. I was one myself. Until I figured out – thanks to you! – that it is none of my business – even though I love my church and our Bible as much as you – to tell others how to pray or what to think… *(looking at* **ANNIE***) or especially, what to wear!*

LUCILLE. I have never –

VERA. *Plus,* it is one thing to try to use your influence to sway us. It's a whole different thing to sweet talk a bunch of men to get your way. Put down your Bible, Lucille…pay attention to what's going on in the world –

LUCILLE. Well…

VERA. Men have been running things into the ground from the beginning of time. It is high time things change.

OLENE. Bite your tongue, Vera. Without men, I'd be nothing. *(smiling as she does a quick dance step)*

VERA. Well, as far as I'm concerned, Olene, they and their inflated egos and undersized… *(hesitates saying the word she'd like to say)* minds can go to H-E-double –

LUCILLE. How dare you use that language!

EDITH. Vera – !

VERA. And until you apologize to your sweet daughter-in-law here or answer her question in a way that makes some sense, you can also go to –

EDITH. *Vera, no more!*

VERA. Oh, I am not near through, Edith.

EDITH. Yes, you are! Because now it's my turn. We've been dear friends for years. Haven't we?

VERA. Thirty-plus years. Yes we have.

EDITH. And I've stood here patiently most of those years listening to you carry on about men –

LUCILLE. "Men are evil." Oh, I know the speech too, Edith.

EDITH. All the time, wondering who is this woman talking about?

VERA. *Men*, Edith!

EDITH. All of them – in one pot. Is that it?

VERA. Well…I suppose there are a few exceptions –

EDITH. Oh?

VERA. Well…Charlie I guess.

EDITH. That's nice to know.

VERA. And my Harry…I guess he isn't half as bad as I make him out to be…some of the time

EDITH. Uh-huh. And your three sons – ?

VERA. I wasn't including them, of course.

EDITH. So there are exceptions to the rule?

VERA. Well, yes…I guess…a few maybe…some…

(*Edith smiles at* **VERA**. *She made her point and* **VERA** *knows it.*)

EDITH. Now, it's your turn. Lucille. You said you believe God tests us.

LUCILLE. We're being "tested" this very minute, Edith!

EDITH. I don't believe that. And neither did Charlie. Life is what tests us. In turn, a loving God gives us everything we need to deal with the changes going on in our lives, even when they're awful…like our church burn-ing, Charlie dying…your organ being destroyed, Mae Ellen, and you feeling alone and afraid…you, Annie, living in a strange town while the husband you love and worry about is somewhere you don't want him to be…Olene coming home to Ivy Gap, finding noth-ing's changed…Vera, desperately wanting us to have a bigger role in things, only to discover our church and society aren't ready for that yet –

LUCILLE. And me, Edith…?

EDITH. In addition to worrying yourself sick about David, I think you're afraid your church *is* changing. You've appointed yourself its great protector –

LUCILLE. Well…

EDITH. I had such high hopes for this "show"! Oh, I know, Lucille, you hate that word, but that's what it would've been…a way for us to *show* we're strong. To *show* we can rise above all the bad things happening around us..at the same time raise a little money that just might've made our church whole again. Who knows? Maybe it was God's way of helping us deal with everything bad that's happening in our lives. Instead, it's divided us when we need each other more than ever. Now, we've got family member against family member… *(looks at ANNIE and LUCILLE)* neighbor against neighbor… *(turns to LUCILLE and VERA)* friend against friend… *(now at MAE ELLEN and OLENE)* The only thing I know for sure is that is *not* what God had in mind!

(Silence as the women look at one another, reflecting on what EDITH has said. Once again, they're an unhappy looking group. After a long moment, MAE ELLEN closes the lid of her piano, slowly rises and begins to cross from the piano to the door to exit.)

OLENE. Mae Ellen…

(MAE ELLEN stops but doesn't turn back to OLENE.)

If you see a good-looking guy out there wearing a tool belt, I hear he's dying to talk to you.

MAE ELLEN. *(unconvinced)* I'm sure he is.

OLENE. Of course, I wish it were me he wanted to talk to me…spend time with –

MAE ELLEN. I've seen you together, Olene!

OLENE. Until the girl – who thought she was something special – got reminded again that good guys prefer substance over splash.

(MAE ELLEN's shakes her head, takes another step to exit.)

You won't listen to that, maybe you'll listen to this.

(MAE ELLEN stops, but doesn't look back at OLENE.)

Once upon a time – a long way from here – I fell for somebody a lot like Reed Hennings. Before I could say Las Vegas, we were married.

(**MAE ELLEN** *turns back to* **OLENE**, *suddenly interested.*)

OLENE. That surprises you, huh? A girl from Ivy Gap runs off to the sin capital of the world…that's what it is, right, Lucille?…Marries a terrific guy, settles down, lives happily ever after. Maybe that's the way it happens here – God, I hope so – but not out there, not when one of them thinks fame and fortune is just around the corner.

EDITH. Maybe this isn't the time, Olene…

VERA. (*understands* **OLENE** *needs to talk*) Let her talk, Edith.

LUCILLE. He left you, didn't he?

OLENE. And I didn't know what I'd lost. So I kept looking, kept marrying other guys – two others in fact. But I never found what I had had.

(*All – even* **LUCILLE** *– look at* **OLENE**; *they realize her pain.*)

So, Mae Ellen…if you see a tall, good-looking guy out there, maybe you don't want to walk away. Maybe you could smile at him or something. Okay?

EDITH. (*speaking to God, almost to herself*) Oh, Lord. I do believe *You've* done it again.

(**MAE ELLEN** *opens the door, looks out, then smiles and meekly waves to an unseen someone.*)

OLENE. Something else, Mae Ellen…

(**MAE ELLEN** *– still in the doorway – turns back to* **OLENE**.)

Since I've managed to depress everybody, maybe we should put on a little something to lift spirits. Considering it's…(*looks at* **LUCILLE**, *managing to smile*) now or never.

LUCILLE. How can you call yourself a Baptist?

OLENE. (*defiantly at first*) Well, I can't be Presbyterian,

Lucille. I can't be something I can't spell. And I'm not Methodist because I refuse to sit while singing "Stand Up For Jesus." So, I'm Baptist because...well, I guess... *(almost as a revelation, emotionally)* because this...feels like home.

(LUCILLE looks at OLENE, dumbfounded at her confession.)

VERA. Sit down, Lucille.

LUCILLE. You can't talk to me like that.

EDITH. *Sit down, Lucille!*

(Reluctantly, LUCILLE finds a chair and sits. At the same time, a more enthusiastic MAE ELLEN makes her way to the piano where she sits.)

OLENE. Annie, would you be brave enough to join me up here maybe?

(ANNIE looks at LUCILLE, then bravely proceeds to the stage.)

EDITH. You, Olene, give meaning to that old adage..."No matter how serious things are, everybody needs a friend to act goofy with." Now, I'm trusting you...

VERA. I can hardly wait to see this.

(OLENE nods to MAE ELLEN who – back at the piano – plays the opening notes of "Alexander's Ragtime Band," doing so with an added flair that reflects her feeling of "victory." After the musical introduction, OLENE sings:)

OLENE.

COME ON AND HEAR, COME ON AND HEAR, CHARLIE'S ANGELS BAPTIST BAND.
COME ON AND HEAR, COME ON AND HEAR, WE'RE THE BEST BAPTISTS IN THE LAND.
WE CAN PLAY AN ORGAN SONG THAT MAKES YOU WANNA GO TO CHURCH,
SO HOLY THAT YOUR GONNA WANNA OPEN UP YOUR PURSE.

> WE'RE JUST THAT CHARLIE'S BAND WHAT AM, OH, HONEY LAMB!

(OLENE steps from the microphone, allowing ANNIE to take her place. She sings these words to the music, an act that greatly displeases LUCILLE.)

ANNIE.

> COME ON ALONG, COME ON ALONG, LET ME TAKE YOU BY THE HAND.
> COME SEE EDITH, COME SEE EDITH, SHE'S THE LEADER OF OUR BAND.
> ONE-HUNDRED YEARS AND COUNTING, AND THE BEST IS YET TO COME.
> WE HAVE THE JOY AND WELCOME YOU, NO MATTER WHERE YOU'RE FROM.
> WE'RE JUST THAT EDITH'S BAND WHAT AM...

ANNIE & OLENE.

> OH, HONEY LAMB!

EDITH. Stop the music! *(The music and song stop. Silence as everybody looks at EDITH.)* Is that it?

OLENE. Hey, we know we're not ready for Broadway. *(looks at VERA, a smile on her face)* Or, are we, Vera?

LUCILLE. The costumes, Edith. The music. Did you listen to the words?

EDITH. Disgraces to God.

LUCILLE. Yes. Yes.

EDITH. The Bible says as much.

LUCILLE. In Leviticus...Deuteronomy –

EDITH. Corinthians, too. "Women should be silent in the church...

(LUCILLE also knows the verse and she and EDITH repeat it in unison.)

EDITH & LUCILLE.

> "... For they are not permitted to speak, but should be submissive."

EDITH. Thank the Lord none of us – including you, Lucille – has ever uttered a word at the First Baptist Church of Ivy Gap –

LUCILLE. *(knows where* **EDITH** *is going)* Edith –

EDITH. We're also told – now, tell me if I'm wrong, Lucille – to give away all of our possessions. Has anybody here done that yet? Other than Lucille, of course. What about an "eye for an eye?" Next time I get mad, y'all better look out – no telling what's coming your way. Or slavery…last I read, Lucille, it's okay. Actually, it's expected, so we are way behind times here.

LUCILLE. Edith, you know you can't take *everything…(hesitating)*

EDITH. Literally? Is that what you were about to say?

   *(**LUCILLE** is silent, aware she's met her match.)*

Nobody respects the Bible more than we do. However, that doesn't keep some of us from picking and choosing. Reciting whatever serves our purposes and ignoring the rest. Have I figured it out, Lucille?

   (Another silence as **EDITH** *and* **LUCILLE** *look at one another.)*

Hey, we all do it. Some of us just a little more than others.

VERA. Look at it this way, Lucille. Either Edith's right…God looks the other way when it comes to some of the Old Testament rules we grew up accepting. Or she's wrong. In which case I have the sneaking suspicion you'll be sitting in Heaven reciting chapter and verse to yourself.

LUCILLE. *(less than convinced but backing down for the moment)* I should know better than argue religion with a dear friend who's addicted to…silly hats –

VERA. *(removes her bright red hat that looks like something members of the "Red Hat Society" might wear one day)* Hey. Who knows what I may have started here?

LUCILLE. Or with a preacher's wife who's something extra special...*(looks at* **EDITH**, *smiling)*

EDITH. Then come here, Lucille...give this *semi*-Bible-thumping Baptist a hug.

*(***EDITH*** *opens her arms to* ***LUCILLE*** *who returns the hug.)*

VERA. I believe Edith's back to being Edith.

EDITH. Olene. Are there any other surprises? Something else I should know?

OLENE. Well...*(disappointed there isn't more)* No. Unfortunately.

EDITH. Then I believe it's about to be "Showtime at First Baptist." Which I know Charlie's gonna love. Okay with you, Lucille?

*(***LUCILLE*** *doesn't quite know how to answer.)*

ANNIE. It'll be okay...I promise...*(warmly)* Lucille.

LUCILLE. Well, I suppose it won't kill me, Edith. Not right away anyway.

EDITH. Good. Because if any church needed something to lift its spirits and raise a little money for things like Wurlitzer's, it's First Baptist of Ivy Gap. Whatdaya think, Mae Ellen?

MAE ELLEN. The bigger, the better, the louder!

OLENE. What about the deacon board?

VERA. Tell them to talk to me.

EDITH. Uh-uh. They owe me big time. Who else in the one-hundred-year history of this church has chaired 139 committees...not counting this mischievous little gang of ours?

OLENE. Oh, I believe there is a God!

VERA. And just maybe...She's a woman!

*(***VERA*** *looks at* ***EDITH*** *who isn't buying what* ***VERA*** *has just said.)*

Well, a girl can hope. Can't she?

(MAE ELLEN and OLENE celebrate EDITH's decision. After a moment, MAE ELLEN plays the opening notes to "Alexander's Ragtime Band." As she does, ANNIE joins OLENE behind the mike. Along with MAE ELLEN – who chimes in from behind the piano – the three-some sing and dance with an extra measure of gusto, putting on a bit of a show in the process.)

OLENE, ANNIE & MAE ELLEN.

COME ON AND HEAR, COME ON AND HEAR, CHARLIE'S ANGELS BAPTIST BAND.

COME ON AND HEAR, COME ON AND HEAR, WE'RE THE BEST BAPTISTS IN THE LAND.

AND IF YOU WANT TO HEAR THAT ORGAN PLAYED A–GA–IN *(three syllables).*

GET OUT YOUR MONEY, GET OUT YOUR MONEY, 'CAUSE WE'RE THE BEST BAPTISTS IN THE LAND!

(MAE ELLEN continues to play the music while OLENE and ANNIE hum the words and continue their gyrations. At the same time, EDITH, VERA and, yes, even LUCILLE – if one were to look closely – sway to the beat. As they celebrate, EDITH looks heavenward, a smile on her face. No doubt she's imagining Charlie's approval of the performance, a thought that gives her great comfort. Lights dim slowly to black. As they do, perhaps we hear an upbeat version of the hymn "Give Me That Old-Time Religion.")

End of Play

A NOTE ON CURTAIN CALL

As the curtain call concludes, directors may want to encourage the cast to clap and sing the word to the music that accompanied their call (in anticipation the audience may want to join in). The words are:

GIVE ME THAT OLD-TIME RELIGION.
GIVE ME THAT OLD-TIME RELIGION.
GIVE ME THAT OLD-TIME RELIGION.
AND IT'S GOOD ENOUGH FOR ME.

IT WAS GOOD ENOUGH FOR OUR MOTHER.
IT WAS GOOD ENOUGH FOR OUR MOTHER.
IT WAS GOOD ENOUGH FOR OUR MOTHER.
AND IT'S GOOD ENOUGH FOR ME.

(REFAIN)

IT WILL TAKE US ALL TO HEAVEN.
IT WILL TAKE US ALL TO HEAVEN.
IT WILL TAKE US ALL TO HEAVEN.
AND IT'S GOOD ENOUGH FOR ME.

PROPERTY LIST

Table cloths (white)
Vera's hats (five as described)
Folding tables
Folding chairs
Podium
Potted plants and helium balloons (optional)
Banner (First Baptist of Ivy Gap...1870 – 1970)
Broom
Cake (decorated with large pink flowers)
Paper plates
Plastic forks
Paper napkins
Magazine
Pen and writing paper
Tray with tea pot and two cups
Small Table
Choir robe
Grocery bags
Bag of pork rinds
TV dinner box
Packaged dessert (boxed)
Notebook
Coffee cups, plates, napkins, etc.
Aprons
Piano or keyboard
Microphone on stand
Director's chair
Pad of paper
Raincoat
Gaudy waitress outfit
Packing box
Various items (of Charlie's) to be placed in the box
Old-looking Bible
Newspaper
Table radio
Flapper-like outfits (see description)

SOUND EFFECTS

Organ music
Bolts of thunder
Siren
Paging of a doctor on a PA system
Construction sounds (hammering, sawing, etc.)
Music from the 1960s (heard on radio)

A NOTE ON COSTUMES

In the early 1970s, clothing styles were breaking from tradition; for example, bell bottoms, tie-dyed T-shirts, denim skirts and miniskirts, scruffy scandals, etc., were becoming all the rage.

That said, Edith and Lucille wouldn't be caught dead in any of the above, opting for conservative styles that reflect their conservative values. Olene, on the other hand, dresses like a well-to-do woman from Las Vegas who follows fashion trends; even when situations demand restraint, she edges on the flamboyant.

Annie dresses like a recent college graduate who must balance her preference for style with the expectations of a very conservative mother-in-law. Mae Ellen's choices are consistent with the area's expectations, but with her own sense of style and color. Vera's independent nature is reflected in her choice of ladies hats (she has a closet full) which have become her trademark.

As indicated in the script, several scenes call for more colorful attire; namely, Annie's retro waitress uniform and Olene and Annie's truly flamboyant Las Vegas-like costumes.

Also by
Ron Osborne...

First Baptist of Ivy Gap

Seeing Stars in Dixie

Wise Women

Ruby's Story

Please visit our website **samuelfrench.com** for complete descriptions and licensing information